A Beginning

The Tower and The Eye, Volume 1

Kira Morgana

Published by Teigr Books, 2024.

This is a work of fiction. Similarities to real people, places, or events are entirely coincidental.

A BEGINNING

First edition. June 30, 2024.

Copyright © 2024 Kira Morgana.

ISBN: 979-8224344673

Written by Kira Morgana.

Thank you to all the D&D, RPG, Action Adventure and Strategy Game writers out there. You inspired me.

One

In the North-East of the Heart Kingdoms, the city of Galindren was settling down for the night. The Lamplighters had already plied their trade on all the main roads, and in the shadows the lamps created, the Thieves Guild continued their evening activities by relieving those who strayed into the side streets of any valuables they might be carrying.

High on the central hill, the Palace was ablaze with light.

"I don't want to see a single shadow in this place," King Koric insisted to his advisors, "Burglars and worse lurk in shadows and I don't want *Them* thinking *They* can take up residence in my home."

"I assure you your Majesty, the Sentries on the wall have been doubled and we have three times the normal number of guards patrolling the halls and on all the exits." Lord Garonne said, folding his hands together under the table. The High Steward seemed more than a little ill at ease.

"Father, the servants are having to shift the soldiers around to be able to clean," His son, Prince Loric said, "If we reduced the number a little, say by a third, we would still be as secure, and the staff would be able to work properly."

Beside him, Loric's brother nodded in silent agreement.

"No!" King Koric snapped, "The guards are needed to make sure that you and Korin remain safe. I've lost enough of my family recently as it is."

"Feran and Ingram died because of you Father, not because of the shadows in the Palace," Prince Loric said in a flat voice, "because of your stupid proclamation on us proving our bravery."

"Loric, don't," Prince Korin whispered, "he'll send you off as well."

Loric winked at him.

"They did, didn't they." The king, diverted from the topic of non-existent intruders, focused his gaze upon his sons.

Loric returned the look steadily, noting an odd gold ring surrounding the pupil in his father's normally pale blue eyes. He filed the thought away to discuss with his tutor later, when he managed to track him down. *Silvertree will be shocked that I'm being so observant.*

Lord Garonne frowned, "What has that to do with the number of guards in the Palace, your Highness?"

"Well, I have yet to set off on a quest to fulfil father's edict," Loric shrugged.

The gleam in Lord Garonne's eyes showed that he had caught on. Korin looked a little confused but went along with his older brother.

"I've heard that there has been an increase in banditry on the north west border, Father," Korin said.

Koric hummed as he regarded his youngest son, a tune that sent chills down Loric's spine.

That's the Ballad of Sir Senith. He kept singing that when he sent my brothers off on their quests. I'm sure that it's to do with that gold ring in his eyes somehow. I have to keep Korin safe. Loric raised his voice a little in an attempt to draw his father's attention, "And I've heard rumours of children going missing to the south, along the shores of the Ice Lake; almost a hundred children have disappeared since the last Winter Solstice. There are tales of monsters and demons abounding in that region according to the studies I have been doing."

"That bears investigating, your Majesty," Lord Garonne said.

"But so does the banditry. You never know, it may be those fools of a Ruling Council in Jinran trying to expand their territory." The king shut his eyes and laid his head back on the top edge of his chairback.

Loric exchanged a panicked look with Lord Garonne.

"That is as it may be, your Majesty, but surely the garrisons on the border would have reported an incursion from Jinran," Lord Garonne gestured to the tapestry map of Galivor on the king's study wall.

A BEGINNING

"Not if they had been paid off by the Council of Thirteen," The king opened his eyes.

The gold ring is wider, I would swear it. Loric felt panic settle into his bones with no clear reason for it. *Why has it appeared? Is there a spell is being cast upon him? I need to speak to Silvertree.*

The king laid his hands on the arms of his chair, pushed it back and himself to standing in one swift move. He walked over to the map and stood, examining it with his hands held behind his back.

"Shut up, Korin," Loric whispered, "You need to stay here and keep an eye on him. Let him send me; Grimhelm would never let harm come to me. He'd die first."

Korin nodded, watching his father's imposing figure pace before the map.

The King turned at looked at his sons, "You two, go pack for an extended journey. Lord Garonne will inform you when and where you are going. Dismissed."

Loric stood up, "Very well, Father. Come on Korin."

As the door was closed behind them by the guard, Korin sighed, "I messed up didn't I?"

"A little bit," Loric said as they set off toward the Family Wing, "You're too young to go on a quest. Hopefully, Lord Garonne will be able to either change his mind about sending you or will be able to send a lot of the guards that are lazing about the palace with you."

"What about you?"

"I'll take Grim with me and see if Silvertree or Lady Kalytia are available to join me. I know the Lady usually enjoys our trips together. Silvertree went off to the Black Forest last week to investigate something for his Queen, so it would depend on if he was finished with that," Loric said, hoping that his tutor had completed his mission and was on his way back. "It'll be an easy enough trip whichever way Father sends me."

"LADDIE, YOU HAVE THE brains of an ox at times," Grimhelm Drakesplitter snorted as Loric threw his bags behind the saddle on his mare.

The sun was just rising above the city walls, throwing long black shadows onto the streets. Flocks of birds wheeled above the roofs and behind them in the palace, they could hear the beleaguered servants preparing for the departure of Loric's brother and his escort.

"Why Grim? The Palace has lost two thirds of the soldiers father had insisted on bringing inside and Korin will be well protected by them on the journey north to a non-existent 'bandit' attack," Loric said tying the bags into place, "I thought it was a good idea."

"Aye, but ye should have had a unit or two at least, as the eldest and heir," The dwarf heaved himself onto the back of his pony which whickered and sidled when Grimhelm inadvertently yanked on the reins to stop himself sliding off the other side.

"If there really is banditry or an incursion going on up there, Korin will need the full brigade, not me." Loric mounted gracefully, "I, on the other hand, can command a unit or two from the local Garrison at Pleasemore if necessary."

"So ye don't expect this to come to much then?" Grimhelm wriggled in his saddle and the pony shook its head. "I hae got to get me a more comfortable saddle, this one feels like it's made of Granite from Reldheim."

As with all dwarves he had a short, burly frame, but his long red beard, split into two plaits, proclaimed him to be from Laikholm. His dragonscale jerkin was dotted with steel rivets shaped like crowns and he wore a steel helmet with a pair of Wyvern horns rising from the top. He was also not at his best this early in the morning; his eyes bloodshot and baggy. Loric wondered just how much ale and mead his bodyguard had imbibed in the King's Boot tavern last night.

The Prince grinned, "If you spent more time working the leather, it would be more pliant. Just because you're lazy is no reason to give that poor pony the backache of a new saddle."

"Changing the subject isnae going to work, Laddie," Grimhelm wagged a finger at Loric, "If ye nae think this goin' ta be more than a pretty ride and a holiday for ye, why bother?"

Loric ignored him and urged his mare into a walk, catching the packhorse's lead rein from the stable lad as he passed him, "Let's get going. We have to pick up the Lady on the way past the White Temple."

Grimhelm grumbled and booted his sturdy pony into following the prince's high stepping steed.

SET ATOP THE SECOND highest hill in Galindren, the White Temple of Espilieth sparkled as if a thousand diamonds covered its stone walls. Inside, the Priesthood had been awake since the Sunrise Bell had rung but one of the highest ranking Clerics, Lady Kalytia of Garinor, had awoken much earlier.

She paced around the Garden in the centre of the Temple Grounds, selecting the best sprigs and leaves for her Herb Pouch. Behind her, a Greyrobe Healer took other cuttings from the same plants for the Temple Herbery.

A white robed boy waited for her as she reached the gate into the flower garden. "The Prince has arrived, Lady Kalytia."

She inclined her head, "I thank you Novice. Inform his Highness that I shall attend him shortly. On your way back to him, inform the stables that I will require my mare."

The Novice bowed his head, turned and hurried off.

"Why do you go with him when he rides out to play, Kalytia?" the Greyrobe asked, placing her basket on the ground and glaring at the white and green robed cleric, "He doesn't need you even a quarter as much as the Hospice or the Healer's Ward does."

The young woman paused in selecting a particularly beautiful rose bloom, "Espillia, what would happen to the kingdom if the Heir to the Throne came to significant harm on one of these trips?"

"Korin would inherit I suppose, but we are not supposed to interfere with the running of the kingdoms we live in, Kalytia," Espillia ground her teeth together in frustration, forcing the words out between them as if they were apple pips.

"I go where our Mistress directs me, Healer Espillia," Kalytia's voice hardened for a moment, "We all do," she continued in a softer voice, "and this is where Lady Espilieth sends me."

"Blessed be Her Presence; May it Heal the World," The Healer muttered automatically at the mention of the Goddess' name, "But why not send a Paladin with him? Why a Cleric?"

Kalytia laughed musically, "If I had a silver horse for every time I've asked myself that, I'd be rich enough to buy my own island."

Espillia sighed, her shoulders drooping, "It's so hard to understand the Goddess' wishes though; there are people who need your powers in the Ward!"

Kalytia patted the Healer on the shoulder, "Don't be despondent, my friend. We all serve in the way we are intended to do." She looked at the large bouquet of roses she had gathered, and a small smile touched her lips, "*Tideeh ssen kcisalltles llaflat eptsa lehtl itnu; Tideen ohwes ohtot ecaepgn irbme httel; Tnecsri ehtnis ehtae rbtaht llalae hmehttel; Srew olfes ehtss elbhte ilipseydal.*"

A white haze surrounded the multi-coloured petals and when it faded away, the petals had a gold edging to each one. She handed the bouquet to the Healer, "Place one bloom beside every bed in the Ward and the Hospice and those who sleep near to it will have an easier recovery or passing."

Espillia's face broke into a smile, "Thank you, Lady Kalytia, that will help immensely."

"Now I must join the Prince, or he may think that Our Mistress has forsaken him," The Cleric said.

"Of course," Espillia bowed deeply as the cleric left.

GRIMHELM SANG *Dwarves Dig Deep* to himself as they left the city and rode south into the countryside. Kalytia and Loric rode just behind him, wincing at the off key notes, questionable lyrics and misspoken words.

Eventually Loric, fed up with his bodyguard's taste in music, caught up with him, "There are delicate ears listening to this, Grim. Would you please be quiet for a bit?"

"Aw Laddie am I upsetting yere delicate sensibilities?" the dwarf chuckled.

"I'm used to your caterwauling, but the Lady is a little more refined in her tastes," Loric pointed out.

Grimhelm grinned at him, "Ye'd think she were used to it by now, Lad. Ye ask her to come on every trip ye make out of the city after all."

"Just stay away from the Urakh drinking songs; they might be a bit too much for the Lady."

Grim winked, "I wouldn't dream of it." And launched into the next verse even louder.

Loric groaned aloud and retreated to Kalytia's side.

"Don't worry, your highness, I'm not offended by his song choices," Kalytia said wincing, "It's his inability to hit the higher notes on key which is causing my shudders."

They talked about inconsequential things as they rode, but after midday when the weather turned from cool and cloudy to damp and drizzly, the conversation lapsed, and the three travellers were glad to arrive at Kalorican Village.

"We'll stay here tonight," Loric said as they approached the Inn, "then travel on to Pleasemore in the morning."

"An excellent idea, your Highness," Kalytia said.

"Ye young nobles hae no stamina these days," Grimhelm grumbled, "Why when I was guarding yere Grandpa, he would'ha pushed through the night to get there."

"Grandfather Feldarak was a soldier, Grim, he spent more time in the saddle and planning border battles in a tent, than he did in the palace," Loric snapped, "We don't have to rush."

They stopped outside the inn and a pair of stable lads wearing the inn's livery ran round the side, followed more slowly by the Innkeeper in a waxed cotton cloak.

"Welcome to The Red Devil Inn, my Lords and Ladies, I am Master Ruasin. My boys will take your mounts to the stables; come forth into the warmth of my Inn."

Loric and Kalytia dismounted and retrieved their packs.

Grimhelm stayed mounted, "If it no be a bother, Master Ruasin, I shall supervise. My little lad hae a way of taking a chunk out o'his carers if he no likes them." He patted his pony's soggy neck.

The Innkeeper waved one hand amenably, "Of course, Sir Dwarf."

An hour later, warm, dry and with a mug of steaming mulled cider in hand, the three of them discussed their plans over a simple meal in the corner of the inn's common room.

"Where is Lord Silvertree, your Highness. Did you leave him behind?" Kalytia said.

Loric shook his head, "Once Lord Garonne told me where I was going, I sent him a message via his assistant, for him to meet us in Pleasemore. However, there is no telling when he'll catch up with us."

"Humph. I know the King made him yere Tutor Lad, but he is nae a good companion for these trips," Grimhelm grumped, "I didnae think ye'd want him on such a simple factfinding mission?"

"I've been studying this 'simple fact finding mission' for a while now, Grim," The prince took a long drink of his cider, "Something about it tells me that I'm going to need Silvertree's skills."

Two

I'Mor Barad's rough cut basalt walls rose from the valley at the centre of the Heart Mountains, as forbidding and nightmarish as the wickedness which had once lived within. As the clouds above the mountains lightened with the coming dawn, a red glow brightened the black stone from the highest windows. Had anyone from the surrounding countryside cared to look up at the tower, they would have been warned that once more, the evil had returned.

However, the valley below the tower was awash with snow melt from the surrounding mountains and the only living creatures who dared set foot there were the large flocks of water birds who used the lake and marshland in the valley as a stopover point in their migrations.

And sadly, the observations of duck and geese were unlikely to be communicated to the humans who lived on the other side of the mountains or the Dark Elves who lived in the massive forest to the west.

Inside the room at the top of the tower a figure, dressed in hooded robes of onyx black and dried blood red, sat upon a throne of tarnished gold. To his right, a suit of black armour hung on a stand. The matching helm with a gold crown riveted to the brow sat on a nearby table.

Opposite the throne, a granite pedestal held a large polished basalt Jar. Carved into the front of the black rock, was a face with a single closed eye.

The figure clapped his hands and an ancient deformed Goblin, his livery matching the robes of his master, scurried in through a small door and bowed to the figure.

"We don't have all day," a deep voice admonished the Goblin. "The Aracan Katuvana is in the mood to start some chaos and you stand there bowing and scraping?" The eyelid on the Jar opened and a luminous green pupil slid around to stare at the creature.

The Goblin sighed and bowed, before darting over and picking up the Jar, holding it with the eye forward.

Aracan Katuvana stood and moved to the southern window; the Goblin followed with the Jar.

Despite the distance, the window clearly showed each village and town, their inhabitants sleeping soundly on a clear moonlit night. The Aracan pointed towards the central city, a roiling mass of humanity that never quite slept.

"That is Galindren, Lord," the Jar told Aracan Katuvana. "Capital city of Galivor, ruled by King Koric. My...your control over him is as sporadic as his sanity. He is, at worst, a mildly disturbed monarch who believes his sons are plotting to overthrow him. At best, he's a possible candidate for Custodian Training." The Jar's eye blinked and the lips moved around fangs longer than the Aracan Katuvana's gauntleted hand, which made a circling motion, inviting the Jar to continue in its summary.

"Koric had four sons, Lord. He issued a proclamation that the only son who would inherit would be the one who proved himself the bravest. Currently, the eldest son, Loric, and the youngest one, Korin, are the only candidates. The second son, Feran, was eaten by one of milord's dragons in the Galivorian mountains and the third son was killed by a horde of Goblins from the southern marches."

Aracan Katuvana scanned the kingdom and gestured again.

The Jar seemed to understand and said, "You only have three dungeons remaining in Galivor, Lord. The Custodians who rule them for you are currently following your last orders to remain inconspicuous. Would you like to change this?"

The Aracan Katuvana nodded and ran a hand across the entire view. The window darkened slightly, and three blood red spots pulsed like tiny hearts beating with evil. The Aracan Katuvana looked at each one in turn, considering which to pick.

Finally, he pointed to where a river exited from a large lake located by the western mountains.

The Jar replied, "That is Pleasemore. It is a pleasantly situated backwater village. The inhabitants like to laugh and are unfailingly polite to one another, despite the relative poverty in which they live. The Dungeon here is watched over by Shandsberf the Rotund, a custodian of middling power, average intelligence and an iron fist. It could be the perfect place from which to start our... your return, as none of those who remember us would expect it to be live. An excellent choice, Lord."

As the Aracan turned to look at the Jar, the object seemed to shrink backward into the Goblin's tabard. The goblin took a step back and the Aracan shook his head slowly.

"Of course, it is an excellent choice, Lord. Our agent in the village has reported an influx of strangers in the last few weeks due to the Spring Festival, including the current heir to the throne." The Jar stopped babbling as Aracan Katuvana made a cut-off action with one hand and turned back to the window, zooming the view into the village.

The Jar sighed with relief. *I must remember at all times that I cannot be resurrected without his aid... and he doesn't like sarcasm.* Returning to confinement in the Lava cave below would not help one bit. For a moment, the Eye looked up at the map of the Heart Kingdoms on the wall nearby, it's gaze going to a spot in the forest just west of the Tower where only a star shape indicated that something lay in the area. *This is the year that I must guide him carefully and set my plans in motion.*

The eye swivelled back to where the Aracan was inspecting the village's inhabitants.

LORIC CREPT ALONG THE dank corridor, wiping sweat out of his eyes with the back of his leather gauntlet and fingering the hilt of his blade nervously.

In the side passage a door opened. A long eared runt of a creature with huge eyes and yellow skin slipped through the gap and crept to where the passage entered the first corridor, watching for the human intruder. Its green eyes penetrated the gloom easily, following Loric's progress up the corridor and as he passed the side passage, the creature giggled and slipped back down toward the door, allowing it to swing shut noiselessly behind him.

The torch in his hand flickered as Loric passed a second side passage. A slight breath of air swirled the Prince's red-gold hair as he paused, frowning, and took a firmer grip on his sabre hilt, sliding the blade out by an inch. When nothing appeared out of the opening, he shrugged, returned the blade into its sheath and continued down the corridor.

Loric blinked as the giggle reached his ears, but as he had arrived at his goal, he checked the metal braced door in front of him and ignored the noise.

He tried to open the door. *Damn, it's locked. I'll have to pry it open somehow. Maybe if I can slide something between the door jamb and the locks?* Completely unsheathing his wide, slightly curved blade, he slid it between the door jamb and the door. The sabre slipped and he narrowly missed relieving himself of a few toes.

I need to be able to use both hands. He grunted, raised the torch a little higher and looked around. To the right of the door a skeletal hand projected from the wall, its palm open; to the left, a grinning skull surmounting a shield of bones.

"I wonder," he muttered.

Loric thrust the shaft of the torch into the palm of the bony hand and didn't flinch as the fingers closed around it, holding the torch securely. He went back to prying the door open, a smug grin on his

The barmaid sniffed and returned to the bar, her nose held high. Another barmaid brought the dwarf's ale, and he paid her three copper coins in exchange.

"Grimhelm, you're going to get yourself thrown out if you don't start treating the barmaids more politely." Loric sighed and finished his mead. *Not that they would pay much attention to him; the people around here are too conservative for that.*

"Well Laddie, ye're father doesn't pay me to be nice to bar wenches. Where in Lady Hel's name did ye disappear off to this morning? Ye never get up before dawn, yet when I awoke this mornin', ye're bed was empty!"

Loric sighed and gestured. The barmaid brought him another tankard.

"Grim, I won't be able to prove myself if I go around with you protecting me all the time."

"That's as may be, Lad, but I am oath-sworn to protect ye." The dwarf's voice rose. "Ye should never have left without me!"

I am never going to win this one, am I, Grim? Loric contented himself with a noncommittal grunt and drank some more mead.

A light, floral fragrance drifted around Loric. He smiled, and without looking pulled out the stool beside him. The black haired, green-eyed Kalytia glided down the stairs. Loric watched her entrance avidly. *I wish she hadn't chosen the Priesthood; we could have been married by now.*

"Have you done something wrong, Highness?" she asked in silken tones as she slipped onto the stool.

"Why would you assume that, Lady Kalytia?" he replied, standing and bowing to her from the waist.

"I could hear Sir Grimhelm as I came down, Highness." She looked at the tankard on the table in front of him and one eyebrow rose in concern. "You started out early, I did not see you when I went to the local temple at dawn and Sir Grimhelm's censure was loud enough to wake the town drunk."

She gestured over toward the fire where a bedraggled man in tattered clothing was staring at them. "Your experience must have been...traumatic for you to have drunk so much already," she finished, her nose wrinkling.

"I can handle it. I am a grown man after all; despite what my... bodyguard seems to think." The prince's eyes narrowed as he looked across at Grimhelm.

"Well, you are here on the hunt for adventure, Highness. I cannot see the harm in a little solo exploration." The cleric looked across at the bar. "However, I believe some food would aid our... discussion."

The Innkeeper noticed her, put the glass he was polishing down and strode over. He bowed. "May I take your order for lunch, Revered One?"

Kalytia ordered a light lunch of roast duck, bread and fruit. Grimhelm doubled the order and added Honeycake. Loric finished his tankard and ignored them.

"And his Highness?" the innkeeper asked.

"He'll hae t'same as me, Master." The dwarf shook his head. "I'll stuff it down 'is throat if I hae to."

Kalytia smiled.

"I have an Alethdariel Blue in my cellar, Lady. It would be my honour if you would sample it." The innkeeper bowed again. "No charge."

"I would be delighted to, Master Innkeeper. Thank you," she replied, "And I insist on paying for it."

One of the barmaids brought Kalytia a delicate blown glass carafe of deep blue elven wine and a matching glass goblet. She placed it carefully on the table and curtseyed.

Kalytia handed the barmaid two gold coins, "To reimburse your master for his generosity."

The barmaid took the coin and curtseyed again, before she returned to the bar.

"See Grim? Even the Lady says you are out of order." Loric grinned at his bodyguard and the dwarf rolled his eyes to heaven at the return to the interrupted conversation.

"Where did ye go then, Laddie?" he enquired, sipping his ale.

"I explored the ruins to the northwest of the village. I spotted something odd about them when we arrived, and I wanted to check it out by myself."

"So, you left your bodyguard here while you risked yourself?" another voice asked from the door.

"How else is my Father going to see I'm the best candidate for the throne?" Loric grumbled into his mead as an elven mage with long silver hair slipped easily through the lunchtime patrons to Loric's table.

"Lord Silvertree, I did not think you were going to respond to the Prince's message." Kalytia called to the barmaid to bring another goblet over, "We have been here three days already."

"How could I not respond, Lady Cleric? With the life of the Heir of Galivor in danger?" Silvertree sat gracefully beside Kalytia and accepted the glass of wine she passed him. "I arrived this morning but felt I should pay my respects at the Forest Temple before I joined your party, your Highness."

Loric winced at his tutor's loud voice. Already, several people on the other side of the room were starting to stare at him.

"That's right, elf," Grimhelm growled across the table. "Advertise the lad's presence to the whole village!"

"And were you not doing that by asking question after question of the villagers at the top of your voice this morning?" Silvertree hissed in a cold tone.

"That is enough, gentlemen!" Loric said as he slapped the table. "I am not the official heir until my father declares me so, and as my revered father is as mad as a frog on a Franierens griddle, I suspect I shall never be declared heir."

Silvertree and Grimhelm glared at each other until Loric slapped the table again.

"If you two cannot get along, I shall be forced to make the two of you remain here until you can, no matter where I go."

Silvertree looked at Loric and sighed. "I apologise, your Highness. I shall endeavour to keep my race's natural instinct to expunge this mud grubber under lock and key."

Grimhelm stood up. "Mud grubber am I? Why you stuck up, pointy-eared—"

"Grim!" Loric snapped. "Enough."

The dwarf subsided, muttering unintelligibly into his ale.

"So, what did you find, Highness?" Kalytia asked.

"In the centre of the ruins is a pair of black doors carved with the Tower and the Eye," Loric replied. "All the books I've read say those symbols are used on the doors to the Dungeons of Doom."

"Those dark, depraved places ruled over by I'Mor Barad?" Grimhelm shook his head. "They don't exist. T'is a child's tale."

"I can't believe that my pupil actually decided to study." Silvertree put a hand to his heart. "Are you telling me that you actually did read those books I sent you?"

"I might ha' known ye'd ha' put him up to this, mage," Grimhelm growled.

Loric shook his head. "It wasn't him, Grim. I thought there might be something in the local stories of creatures stealing children and animals. It was my whole excuse for this trip, remember?"

"He asked me about it. I did a little research and discovered that Pleasemore was once the site of a Dungeon." Silvertree shrugged. "I found the books and went back to my own investigations."

Grimhelm snorted into his ale. "T'king sent Loric and Korin out on wild goose chases. I'm surprised tha' young Korin hae no come a cropper yet, but then again he hae a whole brigade with him, whereas Loric here refused even a unit to accompany him."

"Anyway," Loric emptied his tankard and took a deep swig from the new one. "I thought it would be a quick kill-the-creatures quest. I mean, who really believes that the Heart Kingdoms were once ruled by an evil Aracan from that ruined tower in the Heart Mountains?"

"Obviously you investigated." Silvertree prompted the prince, who groaned.

"Well, yes. I discovered a long corridor with two side passages and a strong locked door at the other end. Unfortunately, it had an alarm spell attached to it and I set it off." Loric trailed off, feeling more than a little ashamed. *Should I tell them about the creature I saw? No. Grimhelm would insist on getting men from the local garrison for my protection, then Father would say it I wasn't brave enough to go in alone.*

"Oh Laddie, ye ran away, didn't ye?" Grimhelm shook his head. "No wonder ye're downing strong mead like water, especially this early in th'day."

"I thought survival might be a good idea. Of course, I ran." Silvertree wore a slight smile and Kalytia's face filled with pity as Loric looked at them. "I can't inherit anything if I go the same way as Feran and Ingram!"

"Listen, ye young gold-hungry..." Grimhelm started, a frown gathering in his bushy eyebrows like a thunderstorm over the Heart Mountains.

"Well, would you rather I inherited or Korin? He's fourteen and only wants to study." Loric's voice rose and Kalytia placed a gentle hand on his arm. He got himself under control. "I can't see Korin being able to deal with the Valdierian or the Jinranian, no matter how many books he reads."

Silvertree and Grimhelm looked at each other.

"Aye, ye may be right Laddie," Grimhelm said softly. "The lad be more suited to study with the Mage's Guild, rather than bashing heads along t'border."

"We shall need a specialist then," Silvertree mused and sipped his wine.

"Who would you suggest?" Loric asked.

"Thiert."

Grimhelm's face darkened, and he appeared about to explode. Loric glanced at his friend and shook his head. "Why Thiert? He's the biggest thief in Galindren."

"Precisely because he is the biggest and the best thief in Galindren. We need someone who can disarm traps and open locked doors. I could use my magic, but I only have so much mana I can use each day. Thiert will be able to do it physically."

Loric considered the proposal.

Grimhelm remained silent, his face looking like one of the gargoyles that graced the battlements of the walls around Galindren Palace.

"How will we contact him and what would he want as payment?" Kalytia asked. "I heard rumours that Thiert's special services are too expensive for even the Queen of Alethdariel to afford."

"I can have him here by tomorrow morning. He owes me a favour and will at least come to hear our proposal. It will be up to Prince Loric to persuade him though." Silvertree stretched. "I have travelled a long way today and I would like a bath, followed by an early night. I would suggest that you all do the same. Assuming that Thiert joins us, tomorrow will be a long day."

Three

"Good news, Lord," the carved Jar said from its plinth. The Aracan looked up from the book he was reading and gestured for the Jar to continue. "Pleasemore Dungeon has reported the presence of Prince Loric. He was discovered poking around the main entrance and was frightened away by an alarm trap."

Aracan Katuvana tilted his head to one side and regarded the Jar with a questioning air.

"If milord's minions can eliminate Loric, then Koric will be left with only Korin as an heir. Korin is fourteen, little more than a child, so he should be easy to remove or even easier to control than his father."

The Aracan nodded and rose, returning to the southern windows. Passing a hand over one window, a detailed three-dimensional map of the Pleasemore Dungeon appeared. Inspecting the dungeon's defences for a moment, the Aracan snapped his fingers twice. An image of Pleasemore dungeon's Custodian appeared on the next window.

"Ah, Custodian Shandsberf," the Jar said. "Your Lord has orders regarding the defences of your dungeon and the possibility of an intrusion by Prince Loric, current heir to the throne of Galivor."

"I hear and obey, Lord," Shandsberf replied, bowing as deeply as his corpulent figure allowed.

"Fortify your defences in these places," the Jar said as Aracan Katuvana pointed out several weaker places on the map of the dungeon, "and dig out an unfortified tunnel from here to here." The Aracan pointed to the treasury and torture chamber. "Link it with the Southern corridor."

"I hear and obey, Lord," Shandsberf said. "I have but one question, if I may be impertinent?"

The Aracan nodded.

"What is it?" the Jar said.

"Will that not cause a weakness in my defences? I have laboured hard to keep this dungeon a secret, in accordance with your orders and allowing any to invade will put rumours of our continued existence abroad." Shandsberf seemed puzzled.

"An intelligent question; an enlightened question even, Custodian Shandsberf. Good thinking," the Jar said.

Aracan Katuvana touched a glyph on the edge of the window sill and a whisper of sound emerged from inside his hood. Shandsberf's head snapped round violently, and blood flew from his mouth to splatter against the wall. The Aracan grunted with satisfaction at the spell's result.

"Our Lord does not employ you to think! Do as you are told," the Jar said.

Shandsberf wiped the blood from his cheek. "Yes, My Lord."

"You had better," the Jar said and Shandsberf's image disappeared.

The Aracan passed his hand over the window again and touched a red symbol carved into the lintel. Another face appeared, a man, hooded with a black cloth across his mouth.

"Are you aware who owns your soul?" the Jar asked. The terrified look in the man's eyes confirmed the answer. "Your Lord and Master has some orders for you. You will receive them in the usual manner. Prepare yourself."

The man swallowed convulsively, then nodded before pushing his hood back slightly and closing his eyes. Aracan Katuvana tapped three times on the symbol and passed his hand over the picture. A shimmering haze surrounded the man's head and shoulders. He screamed once. When the mist cleared, the man's face had a tattoo of a thorny branch curling around his left eye and up across his forehead and down the right side of his face and neck.

As Aracan Katuvana watched, the tattoo faded until it was only a thin line of faint blue dots.

"When the tattoo reappears, carry out the instructions that appear in your mind," the Jar said.

The man nodded, shaking visibly as the Aracan touched the red symbol again and the image disappeared. Aracan Katuvana returned to his throne.

※

THE NEXT MORNING LORIC went down to the main room of the tavern to find Silvertree at a table by the fire. Across from him sat a slight man dressed in a dark brown jerkin, a hood dangling from behind the collar.

Loric sat down next to Silvertree and motioned to the barmaid. She came over, took his order for breakfast and returned to the kitchen. The man in brown had deep blue eyes and a crest of red hair standing stiffly from the centre of his shaved head.

"Where's Grimhelm?" Loric asked Silvertree, still studying the other man absently.

"He hath gone abroad this merry morning to gather supplies for our trip," the elf mage replied. "The beauteous Lady Kalytia is in the Forest Temple, preparing for the adventure that lies ahead."

"Silvertree, why are you talking like a bad Valdierian epic?" the man in brown asked.

Loric shook his head and smiled wryly. "What have you had to eat this morning, Silvertree?"

"The usual, Copperleaf berry bread of mine own manufacture and water. Why?"

"I thought so. It's all right, Thiert, Copperleaf berries may increase Silvertree's powers, but they also make him overdramatic . If you can avoid him until the more irritating effects wear off, then you're doing well."

"How do you know my name?" Thiert asked.

"I'm the oldest son of the King of Galivor. It's part of my duties to know who our most able subjects are." Loric smiled and when the barmaid brought his bacon, bread and a pitcher of milk, he handed her a silver coin.

Thiert grinned.

"I also have to know who our 'Most Wanted' are," Loric finished.

"Ah. That would explain it. Why did Silvertree bring me here then?" Thiert leaned back in his chair and crossed his arms with an expectant air.

Loric made a sandwich of the bacon and bread, bit and chewed while he thought about what he wanted to say. Silvertree had dozed off with his head against his high-backed chair. *I still haven't had a chance to talk to him about the gold circle in Father's eyes...*

"The current buzz in Galindren is that your father is more impressed with your brother's bandit chasing than he is with your adventure seeking," Thiert said.

He knows more about me than I thought he would. Loric rolled his eyes and shrugged. "That will change. Besides, Korin doesn't want to be king. He's more interested in his studies, and he's too young."

Thiert made a noncommittal grunt and watched as the prince finished his sandwich and cleared his mouth with a huge gulp of milk.

"I have located an entrance to one of the fabled Dungeons of Doom. The stories suggest that great riches and glory can be won by those who defeat the inhabitants of even one dungeon, let alone all of those that remain undiscovered," Loric drained his milk and refilled the pottery cup. "If the stories are true, then they can't be inhabited any longer."

Thiert's eyes lit up and he leaned forward again.

Loric noticed idly that the thief had a faded tattoo on the back of his right hand and one that ran across his forehead and around his left eye. He couldn't make out what the design was. *Must be something to do with the Thieves Guild.*

"What sort of 'riches' are we talking about?" Thiert asked, trying to conceal his eagerness.

"Well, the legends have it that each dungeon is built around a vein of precious stones and metals. So, it would follow that each dungeon would be full of riches." Loric tilted his head backward to drain the last of the milk from his cup, "Some of them may even be endowed with magical power or blessed by the gods."

"So why do you need me? Silvertree should be capable of handling anything you should encounter." Thiert leant back, but Loric could see his interest in the way that his eyes widened.

"I only have so much mana available before I have to rest," Silvertree said without opening his eyes. "I can't deal with every locked door and trap we may encounter."

"So, you need me to get you into the dungeon?" Thiert frowned.

"Well, we need you to help us get to the centre of the dungeon, yes," Loric replied, looking at Silvertree. The elf seemed asleep, but Loric saw his eyes were open a sliver.

"So, I could name my price then? I have the skills you need, and you have something I need." Thiert smiled.

Loric sat up, lacing his fingers around his empty cup to stop them jittering.

"What would your price be? Obviously you would get a share of the treasure from the dungeon. What more would you want?" He frowned. *He's up to something.*

"If I need gold, Princeling, I steal it or extort it. I have more gold in my account with the Thieves Guild than you have probably seen in your entire life," Thiert snorted.

"What do you want then?" Loric asked flatly.

"A favour to be asked for as and when I choose, and for you to grant as and when you can without asking in advance what it is." Thiert smiled more broadly and Silvertree opened his eyes and sat bolt upright.

"This favour, it wouldn't be anything that would cause harm to anyone?" Loric frowned.

"I don't know," Thiert shrugged. "I don't know what it is yet."

"Then I would have to have some guarantees," Loric replied.

"Fair enough, Prince Loric. What guarantees do you want?" Thiert stretched and lounged back on his chair.

"I will not do anything that would cause harm to the Kingdom or any of the inhabitants."

"That's fair, it'll be a personal favour only," Thiert said, spitting into his palm and holding it out.

Loric returned the gesture, and they shook once.

Half an hour later, Grimhelm returned. "Everything is arranged Loric. Do ye want to go now?"

"Is Kalytia still at the temple?"

"I saw her going into the saddlers. She said she'd catch up with us." Grimhelm looked at Thiert and frowned.

"Hello, Sir Grimhelm. It's been a while, hasn't it?" Thiert smiled at the glowering dwarf.

"You!" Grim spat. "Silvertree never said Thiert was this creature."

Loric must have looked puzzled because Thiert sighed and in a patient voice explained, "I hustled a Dwarf Bar in Galindren about two years ago. Sir Grimhelm lost about two hundred gold pieces, I believe. Of course, I didn't use my real name when I did it, so he couldn't find me to get his money back"

"'T'was three hundred gold pieces, Thief." The dwarf had drawn the huge war hammer that he wore across his back and looked menacingly at Thiert.

Thiert shook his head and resignedly pulled a very large money bag from his belt. He began counting out gold pieces. By the time Kalytia joined them, the slender little man had six stacks of gold coins in front of him.

"...two hundred and ninety-eight, two hundred and ninety-nine, three hundred." Thiert peered over the stacks to find himself the focus of most of the eyes in the room. "There you go, Sir Grimhelm. Three hundred gold pieces. The exact amount of gold you invested in my little scheme."

Grimhelm pulled out a small, grey stone cube and waved it slowly across the pile of gold. The cube began to glow red.

"A metal sniffer?" Thiert protested. "Do you not trust me, Sir Grimhelm?"

"Not as far as I could throw ye," the dwarf muttered as the cube brightened to a gold colour and beeped. "Thank ye for being honest. Ye must be feeling faint from the experience." The dwarf finished and put the cube away. He pulled a money bag with a Dwarven symbol imprinted onto it and began to sweep the gold into the bag. The neck of the bag flared with a gold glow as the coins tipped into it.

Loric watched amazed, as the whole pile disappeared into a bag that looked like it could hold only 100 coins. "Well, now that's settled, shall we get going?" he asked.

※

OUTSIDE THE INN, A group of older men had gathered. As Loric and his companions left the Inn, the men advanced upon them.

"Lord, please, don't go into that place again," One man, wearing a gold and silver chain stepped forward, "You are the best hope our people have of a future and no one who has gone into those woods has ever come out alive."

Before Loric could say anything, Silvertree smiled and bowed. "Worry not, Mayor Heinlin, the prince is well protected in myself and Sir Grimhelm."

"That's as may be, Ser Mage, but ye've not seen the creatures which lurk in them woods." Another man, wild of hair and stinking of apple brandy threw himself forward to grab Silvertree's robe. "A devil demon stalks the shadows and foul stenches emanate from holes in the earth. Beware!"

Silvertree untangled himself from the man and smiled gently, "I thank you for your concern, Gentlemen of Pleasemore, but we shall be fine."

Kalytia whispered something and the man straightened. He looked embarrassed and trundled back into the group, pushing his way through to the back, "Espilieth protects us, good Sers. She shall see that no harm comes to any who enter."

The Mayor nodded and sighed. "Fare thee well, then, my Lords and Lady."

The men shuffled their feet and called out their good wishes as the group set off.

Four

Pleasemore lay beside the Ice Lake; a long, clear, freshwater lake fed by the mountain streams that tumbled from the southern mountains. The surrounding farmland was lush and productive, and as they left the village and walked along the shoreline road, Loric took a deep breath of some of the freshest air he'd ever experienced.

"Maybe once all this is over and done with, I should have a manor built in this area," Loric glanced back at Kalytia who was walking with Thiert. Grimhelm brought up the rear, keeping an eye on the countryside and Thiert with equal alertness.

"It certainly is a peaceful place," Silvertree said.

"It would be a good place to bring up children," The prince mused, "Away from the machinations and politics at court."

Silvertree supressed a smile as the prince glanced back at the beautiful cleric again, "And who would you marry? You are a Prince after all. Your father would expect your bride to bring something with her to the kingdom; a treaty perhaps or great wealth at the very least."

"I'm sure I could find someone."

A husk of Jackalopes, startled from their morning repast by the group's passing, raced along the water's edge. A long purple tentacle with green suckers beneath snapped out of the water and captured a jackalope, dragging the squealing creature under.

"Life in the country is not without its dangers, it would seem," The mage noted.

"When has life in the palace been safe?" Loric grimaced, "At least the hunting is good out here." He gestured at the Jackalopes who had dashed to a safe distance from the lake and were settling back down to their breakfast.

"And what of the stories of the stolen children?" Silvertree said.

"It's something to occupy my time with," Loric's gaze wandered back to Kalytia, and he tripped over a stone in the path.

Silvertree caught him before he fell and shook his head, "How about we concentrate on the task at hand, rather than the future, your Highness?"

"My father sent me on what he believes to be a fool's errand, Silvertree. I have seen enough of that dungeon to know there is more to it than that," Loric chose his words carefully, "He wishes me to die and Korin to inherit because Korin will be more malleable that I."

"I think you misjudge your brothers abilities, Highness," The mage replied, "Besides, that doesn't sound like the King that I tutored as a boy. He would never deliberately put his sons at risk."

Loric snorted, "You've been away from the palace for too long, Silvertree. Father has completely changed. I even suspect that he has had a spell laid upon him by some maniacal force; a spell that makes him do and say things that he normally would not."

"You've read too many stories, Loric," His tutor's tone was severe, "The only person in history who would have been able to do such a thing, died a hundred years ago."

"Yet I saw that golden ring in his eyes. The stories all say..."

"Now that's enough of that, Highness. Clearly I will have to take your education in hand once this journey is over; allowing you too much free study has warped your investigative faculties and analytical skills," Silvertree snapped.

Annoyed, Loric fell silent.

An hour's walk north of the village, a woodland had grown up, looking out of place against the surrounding farmland. A stout dry stone wall divided the fields from the trees, the track they followed taking a sharp turn to the right and following the route of the wall rather than cutting through it.

"How are we supposed to get in there?" Kalytia asked as they walked alongside the wall.

"There's a broken bit just up here," Loric said. "Looks like a bull or something knocked it down."

"You sure it was a bull?" Thiert cleared his throat, looking around at the wide, hedged fields.

"The field opposite it..." Loric pointed as they came parallel with the tumbled stones, "...has a cattle herd in it."

Near the fence dividing the track from the field, a large red coated bull snorted at them.

Thiert jumped, "Why does everything in the countryside have to make noises?"

"'Tis but nature, friend Thief," Silvertree said.

Grimhelm coughed hard, covering his mouth, his eyes suspiciously bright.

"Can you tell it to shut up then?" Thiert said as he scrambled over the wall.

Loric followed with Kalytia, helping her down on the other side, while Silvertree and Grimhelm climbed.

Inside, the ground beneath the trees was overgrown. The undergrowth consisted chiefly of brambles, stingwort and stinkweed, with large brightly coloured toadstools clustering around fallen trees and rotting stumps.

"This place is creepy," Thiert muttered.

"Ye'd find anywhere without walls creepy," Grimhelm snapped. "Be silent, I feel eyes upon us."

"Don't be daft, Grim. It's a wood, of course we're being watched; by squirrels, deer, rabbits, birds—" Loric trailed off in his recitation, unable to think of anything else that could be around them.

"Don't forget the trees, Loric," Silvertree smiled and gestured around them, "The trees have eyes too."

"As if that makes me feel better," Thiert's eyes darted around him.

Kalytia and Loric exchanged an amused glance.

They made their way into the wood. Eventually the trees thinned, and sky appeared above them.

Loric led the way to the dungeon entrance, weaving through the ruins toward a massive tower that had lost its upper reaches in some storm or battle hundreds of years past. He scanned the area, peering into the trees sprouting between the stones, his hand slipping to his hilt.

"It's noon. Birds should be flying around. Why is it so quiet?"

"Maybe they know we're coming," Thiert quipped. When no one laughed, his smile faded, and he frowned. "Don't tell me you've already been in there."

"How else do you think I know what's inside," Loric muttered.

They reached a large ironbound oak door let into the side of the tower. Loric stopped in front of it.

"This be the place then," Grimhelm snorted. He looked closely at the stout oak branch Loric had shoved through the handles, "Nae one hae been through here since ye left."

"There is usually more than one way in and out of a dungeon," Thiert pointed out. "It could be that the inhabitants just didn't use this door."

How does he know that? Loric walked up to the door.

Grimhelm scoffed, "Pshaw! There be no creatures here. T'is just a folk tale."

"I remember seeing a small creature with green eyes as I left." Loric frowned as he examined the symbol on the door. The steel design had been inlaid into Ironwood and surrounded by gold. *I wonder why the local bandits haven't pried this gold out yet?*

"Just ye're imagination, Laddie."

"Were there any traps in the main corridor?" the little thief asked.

"No."

"Well, I'll go first anyway. You brought me along to sniff them out, after all."

Loric removed his temporary lock, tossed the branch aside and opened the door.

The long corridor was as dank and dark as it had been before. Thiert really did sniff out the traps, his crest quivering as he darted around. He spent a lot of time running his hands over the walls and peering at the floor.

"Can ye nae go any faster?" Grim muttered as Thiert disarmed and carefully wedged shut a pitfall trap to allow them to move forward.

"Aye I could, but then ye'd probably get yereself killed." The thief retorted.

The dwarf growled angrily at the mimicry and would have launched himself at the thief had Loric not grabbed his friend's shoulder.

Thiert bowed to Loric. "If your Highness will advance?"

Grimhelm growled again and marched past Loric, muttering into his beard. Before Thiert could get ahead of him, his foot broke a hair thin string stretched across the passageway.

A pair of humongous swinging blades swishing through the air in front of them. Thiert yanked the dwarf backward, but not before the razor sharp blades had trimmed several long protruding hairs and taken a thin layer of skin off the tip of Grimhelm's nose.

"By Tyr's nose hairs!" the dwarf gasped, "I could hae been sliced in two."

Loric sighed. "This is why we asked Thiert to join us, Grim. I don't want to lose anyone in here."

Kalytia laid her hands on Grimhelm's cheeks and smiled at him, "Shall we restore those handsome looks?"

A white glow spread across his face and when it faded the injury had healed.

She stepped back and he grinned, "Thank ye muchly, Lady Cleric."

The next trap was a set of spikes that erupted from the floor with such considerable force that Thiert turned to glare at the prince in the light of the mage globes Silvertree and Kalytia had produced.

"No traps, eh?"

"Well, there weren't any when I came in here yesterday. The only trap I encountered was one that set off an alarm. That was when I decided that going in by myself was a bad idea."

"Just as well ye did, Lad," Grimhelm growled, hefting his war hammer.

Thiert frowned and produced what looked like another mage globe. He whispered something to it and made it glow a vibrant orange.

"A Trap Hunter!" Silvertree gasped, "Only one Mage in Alethdariel is strong enough to make them, my Mentor…"

"Eliethor," Thiert said with a smile, "She owed me a favour. This is part of what I asked for."

Silvertree sighed, his envy evident.

Thiert whispered to the globe again. It lifted off the palm of his hand and floated down to a foot off the floor and in front of him.

They crept along behind the Trap Hunter. It indicated nothing untoward for another half an hour. Then, as they approached the crossroads, Thiert had the globe hover in the centre of the crossing passageways. It paused and the glow changed to green. Thiert whispered something to it and the glow became white with a green flashing centre.

"A poison gas trap," Thiert smiled.

Loric tensed at the satisfaction in the thief's voice. *He's happy to find a trap; Why?*

Thiert retrieved the Trap Hunter, holding it lightly as he considered the problem.

"How do we disarm it?" Loric asked, but it was Silvertree who answered, after rummaging in the bag on his shoulder.

"Put these across your nose and mouth," he said, tossing a red coloured mask to each of the party.

Loric slipped the band around the back of his head and fastened the laces at the nape of his neck. "What now?" he asked.

"Stand back," Silvertree said. He waited until they retreated a good six feet up the corridor, then began to speak in High Elvish.

"Air Golems," Kalytia said with approval.

Six misty-grey figures, twice the height and width of the elf appeared around him. Silvertree moved away and rejoined the party as the Golems began to advance into the centre of the cross. One of the Golems stepped forward and there was a click. A canister rose from the floor and spun, releasing a fine mist of green glowing gas that shrouded the Golems. The creatures stood there for a long moment, and then one by one they began to fall. It took four golems' deaths before the canister stopped spinning, and the other two died before the canister sucked the remaining gas back into it and dropped into the floor, spent.

Carefully Thiert advanced and sent the orange glowing Trap Hunter into the crossroads again. It indicated no trap in the centre, but when the thief directed it up the other tunnels, the Trap Hunter told them there were more spike traps, just inside each route. Thiert determined where they were and disarmed each one quickly.

"Now which way?" Grimhelm asked Loric, when the thief rejoined them.

"The alarmed door I found was straight ahead by about twenty more feet."

"Won't they be expecting any intrusion to come through there?" Kalytia sounded nervous.

"Aye, Lady Cleric, they would," Grimhelm answered. "'Tis the normal defensive layout for herding intruders."

"They might be expecting us to take one of the side passages instead," Loric said. "After all it would make more sense to avoid a known trap."

"I can disable an alarm trap in my sleep," Thiert scoffed.

"I meant the defensive layout, Thiert. Not the alarm on the door."

"Besides, they'll have alarms on all the doors," Grimhelm told the thief.

"This is getting us nowhere." Silvertree sighed. "Leave it to chance."

"How do we pick, ye high nosed…?" Grimhelm tailed off as Loric gave him an angry look.

"Lady, if you would pick for us?" Loric made a half bow.

Kalytia rolled her eyes at the ceiling, then squeezed them shut, muttering in Elvish as she gestured at each passage in turn. She finished up on the centre passage.

"Happy now?" Thiert asked and picked his way around the bodies of the golems.

Silvertree paused and with a flick of a hand, retrieved the mana he'd used to make the golems. The shaped air dissolved soundlessly.

They encountered no more traps along the corridor.

This doesn't feel right. Why aren't there more traps or any creatures? Loric found himself drawing his sabre. *Maybe they want us to relax our guard? Or there's a stronger trap on the door?*

By the time they reached the door, even Thiert was muttering to himself. The Trap Hunter hovered before the end door, a red bell in its centre.

"They re-armed the trap you disturbed then." Thiert neutralized it quickly before he unlocked the door and opened it a crack. "Suppose you want me to go take a look?"

"No, it's too dangerous." Loric replied with a look at his tutor. "Silvertree?"

The mage bowed gravely and whispered, waving his hands around a small space in front of him. A tiny, bird-shaped Air Golem appeared between his hands and chirped quietly. Silvertree sent the bird through the door. It swooped low over Thiert's head, making him duck reflexively and turned sideways to slip through the crack.

"Scared of birds?" Loric asked.

"Been mobbed by them once too often as a kid," The thief straightened. "My mentor would send me to collect eggs to sell in the market. She said that a good thief should be able to steal the eggs out from under a nesting bird without waking them."

"Took you a while to perfect the skill then?" the prince replied, fascinated.

"Not really. The birds would wake up just after I took the eggs and attack me, which would wake up all the other birds and I'd get mobbed."

Loric and Kalytia exchanged amused looks.

"No traps there that I can see through the Golem's eyes," Silvertree said, as the Air Golem slipped back through the door and returned to him. He retrieved the mana again.

Loric blinked in confusion, "Good to know. But... how can you tell?"

"Air Golems can see aethyric disturbance fields." Silvertree explained.

"Stop talking in gibberish, Mage. I hae no inklin' o'what ye're going on about!" Grimhelm said, "An' if I hae nae idea, the Lad willnae."

"Sir Grimhelm, calm yourself," Kalytia smiled. "Lord Silvertree merely said that his Golems can see the field that activates the trap."

"Why did he nae say that then?" the Dwarf grumbled.

Kalytia bit her lip.

Loric coughed. *I can't laugh at him. He's wound up tight enough as it is.*

Thiert grinned at Loric, and the prince almost lost his control over his mirth.

They slipped through and waited, but nothing happened. A new corridor stretched as far as the eye could see in either direction. Thiert's Trap Hunter couldn't detect any traps within six feet of them either way.

"Good place for a break," Loric said brightly, earning himself a glower from Grimhelm. "What is it, Grim? We need to take a break."

"Ye need to toughen up, Lad," Grimhelm shook his head. "T'is only been two hours since we entered this place."

"I agree with you, your Highness," Kalytia said quickly, "I could do with a rest and a drink."

"So could I. I need to replenish my mana," Silvertree added.

That seemed to settle things. Silvertree set up two mage globes on either side of the door and an Air Golem to guard the other side. Thiert sat still long enough to swallow some water and eat some bread. He kept looking around nervously.

This place is enough to make anyone nervous. Loric thought. He looked around the group. *Grim and Silvertree seem on edge as well, but they're always touchy around each other. Kalytia is always calm, no matter where we go.*

Thiert stood up, stretched and moved away slightly.

"Where are you going?" Loric asked.

"I'm going to scout the corridor. Don't worry. If I find anything I'll come straight back."

"I dinnae trust that man," Grimhelm growled as Thiert activated his Trap Hunter and set off up the passage.

"Trust is not the issue, Grimhelm," Silvertree said leaning up against the wall, his eyes closed. "Besides, he's honest."

"Honest!" the dwarf snorted.

"He has given his promise to help and Thiert does not go back on his promises." Silvertree sounded exhausted.

"Are you all right, Lord Silvertree?" Kalytia asked.

"I'm just drained, Lady Cleric. I've used about a quarter of my mana today already."

"Please allow me to wash the tiredness away. I cannot replace the mana, but I can help you feel less worn out."

The elven mage nodded, and Kalytia brought out a small golden statuette of Espilieth, the Elven goddess of Magic and Healing. She knelt beside Silvertree and began to pray, whispering in Elvish.

Loric watched, fascinated. A white glow surrounded her and expanded to surround Silvertree. The mage opened his eyes and looked at the cleric, awe painting his face as if he could hear something Loric could not.

Kalytia kept praying and suddenly the white glow encased Loric and Grimhelm as well. Loric felt the tiredness lift from his muscles, and the swelling on his right knee, a slight injury caused on the way out of the dungeon yesterday, disappeared. He flexed his leg and smiled.

Kalytia finished and the glow drained away.

"Thank ye, Reverend Lady," Grimhelm said softly.

Loric nodded in agreement, "As soon as Thiert comes back from…"

The little thief hurtled into the midst of them.

"Quick, we need to get back through the door," he said, opening the door and sliding through. "Skeletons!"

Without really thinking, Loric followed, then Kalytia and Silvertree. Grimhelm came last and had only just shut the door when the horde of skeletons rushed past, kicking one of the mage globes into the wall and shattering it.

They stood there listening as the skeletons searched the corridor.

Go away. Loric waited impatiently, the sklattering noise the bare bones made on the paved flooring made his teeth itch.

Once all of the undead creatures had clattered back the way they came, Silvertree fashioned his tiny bird-like Air Golem again, which he sent back through the door.

"They're gone, but I will check to both ends of the passage," the elven mage said after a few moments of looking through the golem's eyes. He closed his eyes and relaxed.

Thiert stood with his ear pressed to the door. Loric moved over to him and cleared his throat softly.

Thiert jumped.

"What happened?" Loric whispered, trying not to disturb Silvertree.

"I went up the corridor and round the corner. No traps anywhere, all the way up. I found another door."

"Alarmed?"

"We are in a dungeon, your Highness."

Loric frowned at the sarcasm and Thiert shrugged.

"Sorry."

"Just tell me what happened. Without any embellishment."

"I neutralised the alarm and went through the door."

"What happened to, 'Don't worry, if I find anything I'll come straight back'?"

"I just wanted to check. Unfortunately, there was a guard post on the other side of the door, staffed with skeletons." Thiert shrugged. "I came straight back, though."

"And they chased you. Thanks, Thiert, we were trying to get in without too much hassle."

Silvertree opened his eyes.

"The Skeletons are back on their guard post. There's a locked and trapped door just beyond them. I saw something interesting at the south end of the corridor though, very interesting indeed."

"And what would that be?" Grimhelm growled.

"Dirt. Soft dirt."

Grimhelm's eyes widened. "A new tunnel?"

"Well, that just confirms it," Thiert muttered. "This dungeon is definitely inhabited."

Five

High in the Black Tower, lounging on his throne, Aracan Katuvana watched the Adventurer's progress through a large crystal ball. On a stand beside the throne the Jar glowed gold as it channelled energy into the crystal, powering the Occularo spell held within.

"It would appear they have discovered the presence of the new tunnel, Lord. Do you want your minions to move in on them when they reach the torture chamber, or the treasury?" The jar sounded strained.

The Aracan pointed to a gold coin the dwarf tossed into the air as he walked.

"The treasury then, Lord. Who did you want to use to carry out the final battle, Lord?" the Jar asked, the gold glow fading as it stopped feeding the crystal's spell. The image in the crystal froze.

Picking up a book from the table beside the throne, the Aracan flicked quickly through the pages and found the appropriate section.

"Ah, the Pleasemore Dungeon Profile. Excellent, Lord."

He ran his right index finger down the list of creatures, stopped and tapped four times on one entry. Then he continued for a few lines, stopped and tapped nine times on another entry.

He kept on like this for several moments. The Jar watched and counted, its eye fixed beadily on the page, and once Aracan Katuvana reached the end of the list and closed the book, the Jar summarised.

"Four units of Dark Mistresses, nine units of Dragon Spawn, three Poison Demons, three patrols of Skeletons and Pleasemore's Devil Demon." The Jar paused for a long moment, before it asked "How many Gremlins?"

The Aracan shrugged.

"As many as it takes then, Lord. Superb choices all, may I say. Oh look! The prince and his friends have reached the entrance to the new tunnel."

Aracan Katuvana turned back to the crystal and the Jar fell silent, once more channelling energy into the ball.

"YE WERE RIGHT, SILVERTREE. This is a fresh tunnel," Grimhelm said sifting earth through his stubby fingers. He sniffed the dirt and darted his tongue onto the mound in his hand. "It's been sat here for half a day mayhap."

"I don't like this. It feels like an ambush," Thiert muttered.

"What about that locked door the bird golem found behind the skeletons?" Loric suggested.

"You wanted to get in without any hassle, Loric," Thiert said. "We'd have to fight the skeletons to get to it."

"We've had quite enough fun with skeletons today," Silvertree said firmly.

The thief shrugged. "No argument from this quarter."

"Aye lad. Let their weakness become our strength." Grimhelm stood up, dusting the dirt from his hands. "Surely there'll only be a small show of strength up here to protect t'workers. They will nae be expecting us to enter here when we are so few."

Loric frowned and rubbed his temple. *My head is pounding, and something just feels wrong about this. Is Grim right?* "What about the door in the small corridor off to the west?" he said.

"Are ye determined to nae follow t'advice o'ye're advisers?" Grimhelm growled at him.

Kalytia placed her hands on his head and whispered something. The headache faded and he smiled at her gratefully, kissing her palms in the traditional thanks.

"I want to check that other door first," he said.

Grumbling, the dwarf led the way to the western door. Silvertree knelt beside it and fashioned a snake golem from the handful of earth he had brought with him. They moved back from the door, so they didn't trigger the alarm and the mage sent the snake in under the door. Then he closed his eyes and vocalised what he saw.

"Short corridor ending in a small east-west corridor. I'm going east first. Hmm, chickens. This must be a feeding ground, but... it's so small, barely five paces across. Another passage leading north. Short, into a tiny treasure room."

Loric interrupted him. "Treasure room?"

"Well, it must be, there are gold coins and gems scattered all over the floor. Corridor leading west. Slightly longer than the last one. Ah, this room is clearly a bedroom. There's a throne-like chair and a bed. Passage going south now. Hang on. There's an open door to my right. A strange red glow coming out of it."

"What is it?" Kalytia asked.

"I recognise that symbol. It's a Dark Temple, Lady Cleric. A place of blood sacrifice." Kalytia gagged and went pale. Silvertree continued, "The last room appears to be either a training..." Suddenly Silvertree opened his eyes and swallowed hard, blinking. His hands rose to cradle his head and he gasped for breath.

"What happened?" Loric asked.

"The golem was stamped on?" Thiert hazarded a guess.

Silvertree nodded, unable to speak. Kalytia laid her hands on the elven mage's head and when she finished Silvertree was able finish his sentence.

"The last room is a training room, and it was in use...by a Devil Demon."

"Now who is talking about fairy tales." Thiert scoffed, "That's the sort of monster you get in the stories you hear on Sowain Eve."

The mage groaned. "It stood on my golem and broke the spell; it was real enough."

"Aye thief, Devil Demons are real enough creatures. You humans are too short lived to remember the Black Tower War." Grimhelm said.

"Us humans did most of the fighting and dying as I recall my history lessons." Thiert snapped.

"I'm surprised that a thief would know even that." The dwarf replied, "Ye aren't exactly scholars."

Thiert squared his shoulders, one hand dropping to his dagger hilt and Loric braced himself to jump between them.

"Gentlemen, might it not be better to continue this discussion elsewhere?" Kalytia pointed at the door. "The demon may decide to investigate the noise otherwise."

The dwarf and the thief looked at the door and then each other.

"Aye lady, ye may be right." Grimhelm acknowledged.

They retreated up the southern corridor.

"Thank you, Lady Kalytia." Loric murmered to her as they approached the new tunnel. "I thought for a moment that we may have a fight on our hands."

She smiled.

At the new tunnel, they stopped to organise themselves. Kalytia pulled a wicked looking, slim-bladed short sword from underneath her tabard and as she unsheathed it, a golden flame ran the length of the razor-edged blade. Grimhelm sighed and pulled his war hammer from its sling on his back, rolling his shoulders around and stretching his neck from side to side.

Silvertree spoke a few words in Elvish as he uncovered the end of his staff. The crystal blazed with pure white light, making the mage globe that Kalytia held look dull in comparison.

"I don't like that this is our only option." Loric sounded resigned, and drew his sabre, "I feel like I'm being herded."

"Aye, I know what ye mean laddie, but ye don't want to come up against that Devil Demon wi'oot at least a ten man squad wi ye." Grimhelm said, "This be the safest route."

"I hate walking into an ambush," Thiert muttered drawing two long-bladed knives that gleamed blue in the mage light.

"Look at it this way Thiert. There are unlikely to be any traps or locked doors," Loric replied.

Cautiously they started up the tunnel, their feet making virtually no noise in the soft dirt of the floor. Loric frowned as they came upon a stone wall.

"What's the matter, Lad?" Grimhelm asked.

"This is a fresh tunnel, why is there a stone wall here?"

"I would say because it's the wall of another room," Silvertree said from behind him.

"Could we break through it?"

The dwarf examined it carefully then shook his head.

"Nay. The stone is reinforced with magic laced mortar and even old Bessie wouldn't be able bash through." He patted the head of his hammer consolingly.

They moved on. In the dirt they saw the marks of tiny feet and the occasional hoof or paw print, but no live creatures appeared.

"I really don't like this," Thiert said as they came upon a freshly dug side tunnel. He slid into it, motioning for the rest of them to stay where they were.

He came back shortly after, his face so white that Loric could see his veins.

"Empty. Let's move on quickly."

"Now ye wait just one minute, ye…" Grimhelm started.

"Hold on Grimhelm. What was in there? Could we go through?" Loric interrupted.

"It's not the sort of place that you take a Lady, especially a Lady of Espilieth."

Kalytia frowned. "I appreciate the thought, Thiert, but I'm not that delicate."

"So, you want to walk into a torture chamber? Fine, if that's what you want," the thief replied and turned to go back in.

"No! It's all right." Kalytia turned pale and Silvertree started to move, but she waved him off. "I'm a grown woman, but the thought of all that death and pain makes me feel ill."

"And you carry a sword? What were you planning on doing with it, bless the creatures that attack us?" Thiert sounded rather annoyed.

"It is one of the few Holy Blades of Espilieth. It can do much more than just kill." Kalytia turned away from the thief and said to Loric: "Let's move on. I'm sure if we're quiet enough, we'll be able to get past without alerting anyone who might be in that room."

※

IN THE TOWER, ARACAN Katuvana left his throne and moved to the window. The ancient Goblin once more walked behind him, carrying the Jar. Waving his hand across the window again, the Aracan produced the top down view of the Pleasemore dungeon.

"If you recollect, my Lord, the adventurers are shown as a white line," the Jar said.

The Aracan nodded and touched a small symbol at the bottom of the picture. The map disappeared to show the party in a small circle. Jar and Lord watched as behind the party Gremlins silently faced the walls with granite blocks and laid down flooring. They added a strong door to the torture chamber and put traps around the entrance.

"They have almost reached the Main Treasury, Lord. This should be very interesting." The Jar cackled with delight. "I suggest you activate my... your agent."

Aracan Katuvana nodded and made a complicated gesture over the thief who stood guard at the back of the group, peering around the corner. Despite the lack of sound, the shock of the spell activation manifested in the way the thief clutched at his hand and then his skull.

He dropped to the floor and managed to crawl around the corner before collapsing.

A deep booming laugh echoed around the tower as the Aracan waved his hand over the scene, returning it to its top down view.

"Most entertaining," the Jar remarked.

SILVERTREE SENT ANOTHER earth snake into the room ahead.

"It's a Treasury—piles of gold and precious gems everywhere. Gilded armour and weaponry, in essence a great deal of loot from previous adventurers."

"Any creatures?" Loric asked.

"None. It's safe enough to go into." The snake returned to the mage who dispelled it and absorbed the mana it released.

"This really does feel like a trap. Thiert..." Loric said as he twisted round. He blinked, the thief had disappeared.

Leaving the others at the roughed out entrance, Loric backtracked almost as far as the Torture Chamber.

The Prince found Thiert sitting on the floor with his back against the wall. He'd pulled his hood up over his Mohican and ran his left hand over his right one repeatedly. Either side of him his knives were laid flat and the marks in the fresh dirt suggested the little man had fallen here.

"Are you all right?"

"I'm fine, just... had a bit of a funny turn. It happens every so often. What have you found?"

"A Treasury. There are no creatures in it."

"Have you seen any creatures other than the Skeletons that chased me?"

"No, but what about the Devil Demon Silvertree saw behind that locked door?"

"We only have his word for it and besides he might have seen a statue. Look, Loric. I'm telling you there are no creatures in this dungeon. We should just walk in, get whatever you came to get and walk out again."

"Statues don't stamp on golems," Loric took a deep breath, "What about all the traps we've encountered?"

"They could have been timed ones. Set in motion by your exploration yesterday."

"What about the Skeletons?"

"They're Undead. They might just be remnants of what was here before. Remember it's been hundreds of years since these ruins were standing properly, let alone lived in."

Loric was unconvinced. "The fresh tunnel?"

"The Skeletons could have dug it as a route from their guard post to the south tunnel." Thiert changed the subject. "What was it you wanted to get anyway?"

"Well, the Legends say that the centre of the Dungeon has a large magic crystal in it." Loric sighed. "My father suggested that it would be the only thing he would accept as proof of my bravery and loyalty." He looked at Thiert more carefully. *Something is wrong. He doesn't feel like the same person to me.* He had stopped rubbing his hand and Loric caught a glimpse of the tattoo on the back of it. *His tattoo looks darker for some reason. Maybe it's the light in here.*

The thief saw the direction of his gaze. Collecting his knives as he rose, Thiert stood up. "Let's get back to the others. The sooner you get the crystal, the sooner we get out of here."

Loric nodded and followed him back to where the others were standing, passing around and sipping from one of the water skins. As he and Thiert returned, Kalytia held the skin out to him, a soft smile on her face. He took it gratefully, using the water as an excuse not to speak.

"Where were you?" Silvertree asked "We turned round and you two had disappeared."

"I was dizzy. Loric came to help me," Thiert replied.

"Well now ye're back, we can get on with this," Grimhelm grumbled. "There are no creatures in the treasure room, so we might as well go on in."

Six

They slipped into the room; their weapons held at the ready and paused by the tunnel entrance. After half an hour of waiting, Thiert was the first to sheathe his knives and pull out his treasure bag. "Might as well help myself to some of this, it's just lying around all lonely with no one to spend it."

"The thief has a point." Grimhelm smiled for the first time, opening his tiny money bag and picking up gems from a nearby pile, examining them and putting them in it.

"Gold is too heavy," Loric said. "I came for the crystal."

"Take some gems, Loric. They weigh very little and are worth more than gold," Thiert said.

"I will not profit from the evil that created this horrible place," Kalytia declared, moving to stand beside the northern door leading away from the tunnel.

Silvertree shrugged. "Gems can be cleansed of evil and are more useful as enchantment foci than as money." He, too, retrieved a bag from a pocket in his cloak and began to select the best of them, picking through the pile carefully.

Loric wandered across the room, skirting a large pile of massive gems in the centre, to stand beside the south door. *The books Silvertree sent me were too vague about the dungeons. Why on earth are they here? Was it really the Aracan Katuvana or did some other evil lord create this place or was it something else?* He stared into space.

"I can hear you thinking all the way over here, your Highness," Kalytia said with a tight smile. "What in the Lady's Name are you thinking about that has you concentrating so hard on nothing?"

She's a Cleric of Espilieth. Surely Kalytia would have the answers that weren't in my books. Loric smiled back. "I was just considering the history of this place. Do you know anything about this Aracan Katuvana that was supposed to have existed?"

The cleric's smile disappeared, and she looked sad. "A poor subject to discuss. Especially when we are surrounded by his miasma."

"I don't understand. The books I read all hinted about the legend of The Aracan Katuvana, none of them seemed to be at all certain of the facts," Loric shrugged. "I'm beginning to think the books made the whole thing up. I mean, it could just be the creatures who live here who have collected this treasure and made people disappear."

"He was real. The elves still sing of the horrors inflicted upon the Heart Kingdoms during his terrible reign." Kalytia sighed.

"The dwarves too." Grimhelm looked up from his gem sorting, "It was one of the main reasons that we stayed away from the human kingdoms for so long after the War."

"You trained in Alethdariel, didn't you? And the elves remember more about the Black Tower War than any of the other races of Quargard." Loric darted across to Kalytia. "Please, tell me about it. Why did the Aracan Katuvana build this place? What was his motivation for attacking the kingdoms and why would my father be so insistent that I find this crystal for him?"

Silvertree looked up from his appraisal of a large amethyst. "You were never that interested in the politics of the War when I was tutoring you, Loric."

"Ye're nay as pretty as the Lady Cleric, mage," Grimhelm chuckled.

Kalytia frowned at the dwarf and turned back to Loric. "This is no pleasant tale, Highness. I feel faint just thinking about it."

"You can't be that fragile, Lady Cleric," Thiert interrupted. "Not if you accompany the dwarf to inns and taverns on your journeys."

"Hush, Thiert. The lady is a delicate bloom indeed, but I know something of the rites the priesthood go through and to have survived this far..." Silvertree ducked as Kalytia snatched up a small bag of coin and threw it at him. "Sweet Lady!"

Grimhelm laughed at the mage's expression and even Thiert smirked.

Loric took the cleric's hands. "Please, Kalytia? I just want to know why you feel this ruin is so evil; so, I may counsel my father, the King, on its fate."

She sighed. "Very well."

Loric sat down on a large chest.

"This disgusting place must be one of the dungeons that were built to impose the will of the Aracan Katuvana on the Heart Kingdoms," Kalytia said. "There were at least three in each of the kingdoms; possibly more, and it fell to Ser Senith, a Paladin of the Mother, to cleanse the world of the Aracan Katuvana's evil."

"But why did he do it?" Loric frowned. "Why would one man create such places?"

"Why does anyone attack another? Power, money, or thrills are the usual culprits," Silvertree answered the prince. "There is a story that the Aracan Katuvana had once been High Councillor of Jinran and that he grew weary with the riches of that land and wished to impose his will upon all the kingdoms."

"The true motivations of the Aracan Katuvana are obscured by time, Highness. However, there is one fact which has never wavered in either the minds of the Elves or the Priesthoods." Kalytia looked around nervously. "The evil tainting this place reeks of it and thus confirms all I have been taught; the influence of the Dark Ones is very real and the Aracan Katuvana was sworn to their service."

Loric grimaced. "I was hoping there wouldn't be anything supernatural in this tale."

"It is no tale, Highness, but truth. In as much as my Lady Espilieth is of the Deities of Light and I her sworn cleric, the Aracan Katuvana was the sworn vessel of the Deities of Shadow and carried out their will." Kalytia fell silent.

Loric returned to his post by the southern door, thinking hard. *There must be some kind of spell on this crystal that my father wants. Perhaps it has the power of the Aracan Katuvana in it and he thinks it might help him in his fight with the Valdierian.* He shied away from the thought that his father wanted it for any other reason, but one appeared in his mind anyway. *Maybe he wants to become another Aracan? No, father may be unhinged, but he isn't evil.*

Time stretched out around them. The wealth of the dungeon glittered in the mage globe's magical light and soon Loric had relaxed his guard. He idly watched Silvertree examining an emerald the size of his fist with an eyeglass. Grimhelm had found four matching rubies and was sifting through another pile to find a fifth one, as a wedding present for his sister, he claimed.

Kalytia was the only person who had not relaxed. She was getting more and more anxious as the evil that permeated the stones of the dungeon affected her.

"Please can we get this crystal and get out of here!" she pleaded for the tenth time.

"Just a bit longer," Grimhelm muttered.

"Relax, Lady Cleric. There is nothing to worry about, this place is deserted," Thiert said, grinning at her.

It didn't help.

Loric frowned. Earlier the thief had been advocating a quick get-away, now he seemed content to plunder the dungeon. *What's going on? It's like the treasure trove in here has them hypnotised.* He watched Thiert select his route through the room, over to the biggest pile of gems.

At the very top of the pile was a massive Fire Opal, twice the size of the large emerald Silvertree had in his hands.

"My Gods!" the thief exclaimed. "I have to have that one."

"Be careful!" Loric barked as Thiert reached up, balancing precariously on one foot.

Grimhelm and Silvertree looked round as the rascal got the gem, then tumbled onto the pile of treasure underneath it. He lay there, sliding the gem into his pouch and grinned weakly when he saw them all looking down at him. As he turned over and sat up, the gems behind him slid down and Kalytia saw the top of an alarm trap under him.

"Thiert! Stay still, you've sat on a trap!" she called.

The thief froze. His hood slid back off his head, exposing the tattoo Loric had seen earlier in the Inn and Silvertree gasped.

"A spell tattoo!" The elf moved closer to examine it.

That ink is definitely darker than it was earlier. Loric frowned. "What's a spell tattoo?"

"I sent you books about Aracan Katuvana when you started researching this quest. Didn't you read them?" Silvertree frowned at his pupil.

"Well, sort of." Loric looked down, squirming slightly. "The ones I read had more stories in them than anything else."

"You always were an indifferent student Loric, preferring fantasy to history," Silvertree sighed. "Your brother paid far more attention to what I was teaching than you did."

"Explain it, Mage; don't have a go at th'lad," Grimhelm said slipping a fifth ruby into his pouch and tying it back on his belt.

"When the Aracan Katuvana was in power, those humans who accepted his rule or sold him their soul were tattooed with a thorny branch that extended up their right arm, up their neck, across their forehead and around their left eye." Silvertree turned to look at the thief, considering. "The only difference between the two types of human servants was that those who had accepted his rule had tiny black roses in-between the thorns. Those fully possessed by him had red roses."

Loric looked back at Thiert. The tattoo he had glimpsed on the back of the thief's right hand had been a thorny branch and now that the rogue's hood was down, he could see the tattoo ran up right side of his neck, across his forehead to curl around his left eye socket, just as Silvertree described. There were no tiny black roses between the thorns.

"So, you sold your soul to the Aracan Katuvana, did you?"

"You don't understand. When I was a tiny child, my parents couldn't afford to keep me so they left me on the doorstep of the nearest Guild they could find. Unfortunately, it was the Thieves and Swindlers Guild and though they took me in, the Guild Elders also sold my soul to the Dark Ones to make the Guild rise in status. Two days ago, this appeared." Thiert sounded distraught.

"I knew we couldna trust ye!" Grimhelm snarled drawing his hammer and advancing on the man.

Kalytia went white and took three steps forward, her right hand outstretched as if trying to stop the dwarf from doing anything. Her foot slipped on the gold scattered across the floor and she fell, hitting her head on the floor.

She didn't move.

Silvertree scrambled across to her and Grimhelm turned to help.

Loric could hear something coming from the door behind him. As the noise got louder, a foul stench filled the air. He turned, raising his sabre and shouted "There's something..." but he never finished his sentence.

The south door burst open, and the fattest demon Loric had ever seen stood there with two more behind it. The creature waddled in and Loric backed up as he realised that the smell was coming from the demon. As it advanced, it farted, each step releasing a cloud of gas that made him gag. *Use the gas mask,* he told himself, pulling the red mask from his pocket. One handed, he managed to get it over his head while holding his sabre out in front of him. *Good. Now what do we do?*

Once the demons were in the room, they spread out, not caring what they trod on. Loric didn't dare take his eyes off them to find out what his companions were doing. He brought his shield round from his back and slipped it onto his arm, praying fervently to any of the Gods that might be listening.

The demons roared and shook their heads, rattling the chains and spiked balls attached to their long horns. He backed up further, until he bumped into Thiert who was still half lying on the alarm trap.

"Duck, Loric!" Silvertree yelled and the prince dropped to the floor. A green fireball flew through the air where his head had been and hit the centre demon. It lodged in the creature's stomach for a few minutes and the other two demons crowded round to examine the wound. They appeared puzzled and the injured demon poked at it with one long, dirty fingernail.

The fireball contracted slightly and as Silvertree called out, "Stay down!" it expanded rapidly.

The injured demon was torn into bloody chunks, throwing the other two demons through the air and into the side walls. The audible snap as they hit the walls indicated that their necks had broken. The bodies slid down to lie still on the treasure.

Loric barely had time to blink before a horde of tiny Gremlins wearing dirty red tabards rushed into the room through the east door, cleared up the bodies and rushed away shouting "Hup, Hup, Hup," at the top of their voices through the opposite door. The door slammed shut behind them and they heard a key turn in it.

"Why did they lock it?" the Prince asked no one in particular.

Grimhelm strode over to the door in the north wall and tried it. It wouldn't budge.

"This one is locked too!" he called.

Loric scrambled up, turning to look back at Silvertree and realised that a door had appeared in the entrance to the new tunnel. He dashed over to it, slipping and sliding on the gold disturbed by the explosion of the green fireball.

"Locked!" He looked back at Thiert. "Not inhabited, huh."

The thief shrugged.

"I was going on what I'd seen. I've seen too much nastiness in this world to believe in fairy tales."

"Well, we're trapped. And we still haven't found the crystal," Loric sighed.

"It should be through the south door. All of the books I sent you say that the Crystal is the Heart of the Dungeon, and I can feel the Aethyric field pulsing from that direction," Silvertree said as he administered a healing potion to Kalytia. She groaned and sat up, whispering a prayer, completing the process Silvertree started.

Before the group had a chance to discuss what they were going to do next, the north door unlocked and three skeletons rushed in, screeching.

How can something with no lungs or voice box make so much noise? Loric wondered and set himself to fight them anyway. *If I break them apart enough, maybe I'll find out.*

He never got the chance because Kalytia cried out in Elvish, and a white glow filled the room. The three skeletons tumbled into piles of bones and didn't get up again.

Loric lowered his sabre again. "Thank you, Lady Cleric."

She smiled weakly and passed out on the floor, fast asleep.

"That was a high level spell. I think she'll have to sleep for a while before she can use any more magic." Silvertree lifted her and carried her over to the south east corner of the treasure room. He laid her down behind three large piles of gold and gems and covered her with her cloak.

"Hopefully we can deal with anything else that comes in."

Seven

A rumble and roar from outside the room announced the approach of many enemies. The noise came from everywhere at once and both Silvertree and Grimhelm looked alarmed. Loric moved from door to door rapidly, trying to figure out where they would be attacked from.

He rejoined the others, feeling more than a little worried.

"I'll protect Kalytia and Thiert," Silvertree said, positioning himself so that he wouldn't have to move far to protect them.

Thiert, who was still half lying on the alarm trap, slid his blades free of their sheaths. "Don't worry about me too much Silvertree; even lying down I can still defend myself."

"Grim, you and I will have to keep the area around Silvertree clear," Loric said, "I just hope we don't get attacked from all sides, there are too many doors in this place."

"Aye." The dwarf grunted.

The new door opened and three creatures that looked like a frog and a dragon had mated came in through the new door. They looked around and attacked Loric enmasse.

The prince moved in to engage one, blade held low in front of him. The others appeared to be waiting their turn. *These monsters aren't exactly intelligent are they!* The one in front of him spun on the spot, the spikes on its long tail tripping him.

As he landed in a pile of coins, Grim launched himself at the group, Bessie held out to one side, head down with the wyvern horns pointing at the back of the creature in front of him. "*Airson fuil, urram agus òr!*" he roared and speared the creature neatly with his helm. The thing shrieked, letting out a jet of flame and turned to face Grimhelm, taking the helm with it, wrenching his head to one side for a moment.

Loric surged up, stabbed the creature that had tripped him through the roof of the mouth as it opened it to breathe fire, ripped his blade free and yanked the helm out of the other creature's back. "Thought you might need this." He tossed the helm to Grimhelm as the dwarf despatched it with a mighty swing of Bessie, the side of the creature's skull crumpling like wood.

Grimhelm caught the helm, shook ichor off the horns and slammed it back on his head. "Aye, thank ye lad."

The two of them turned to face the third creature which looked at the remains of its two brethren turned and ran for the door as fast as it could waddle, its tail spikes knocking piles of treasure everywhere in its haste to leave.

"Wise decision." Loric muttered.

As the creature reached the door it was lifted into the air, turned and pushed back toward them somehow.

"That clears up any uncertainty about the status of this place; it's definitely being tended by someone," Silvertree said, "That was deliberate control magic. Stand aside!"

Loric looked round at the mage.

He held a large orange gem that sparkled with energy; a soft red smoke drifted up from it where his hands touched its surface. Silvertree muttered something in elvish and the gem burst into a bright light that illuminated the treasure around him in a wide circle.

The creature paced forward, reluctance in every step. "Grimhelm, hit the gem with Bessie as hard as you can!" Silvertree threw the gem toward the attacker.

Loric moved backward as his bodyguard swung Bessie. The massive Warhammer contacted the gem and smashed it into shards, every single one blazing with light. The creature tried to pull back toward the door, but whatever spell was controlling it, kept it moving forward.

The gem shards slammed into the creature, energy sparkled out from each one covering the creature in a web of energy. It shuddered and shook in a grotesque kind of dance until it fell onto the floor, it's scales rattling against the stone and treasure it lay on.

As soon as it stopped moving, a pair of women in tight leather battle harness pranced in, blowing kisses. Their long hair was tied into plaits that had blades attached to the ends, but they didn't seem to have any other weapons.

"Women? I doubt these two could hurt us." Loric relaxed a little.

Grimhelm laughed. "Aye, Lad. Just turn on ye charm and they'll nae give us any bother."

The women pounced on them biting and scratching with glistening, sharpened fingernails.

"I'm not sure charm would work, Grim." Loric barely brought his shield up in time to fend off one of the women. "They seem to be rather annoyed with us. You don't think they used to be barmaids that you insulted?"

"Laddie, I would ha' recognized them; normal wenches ha'nae use for sharpened nails!" Grimhelm ducked a clawed palm strike to the face, followed up by a steel heeled kick.

The other woman ducked under Loric's shield, reaching for his throat and Loric caught a whiff of something sharp and acrid from her hands. He moved backward quickly. "Grim I think their nails have poison on them!"

Both women shrieked with laughter and doubled their attacks. The two warriors fought back and managed to kill one, as another two cavorted through the door, this time alternating the kisses with fireballs.

"Dark Eye Mistresses? That confirms it; this place is one of the Aracan Katuvana's Dungeons all right," Silvertree groaned. "Only the higher ranking ones were sorceresses."

"Silvertree, you have the worst possible timing for information like that!" Loric raised his shield and looked at Grimhelm. The dwarf nodded and the two of them moved forward carefully, keeping their adversaries at sword's length. However, the three women joined forces, pushing Loric and Grimhelm backward toward Silvertree.

The mage projected a force field around them and with carefully timed attacks, dwarf, elf and human were able to carve the women into pieces. The blood that oozed from the chunks was a deep black and clotted.

The little Gremlin creatures rushed in, grabbed the still twitching remains and ran out. Another six of the dragon-like creatures appeared from the south door, almost immediately after the Gremlins left and this time Thiert had to fight lying on his back.

Loric found himself backed into a corner between a pair of massive gold filled boxes. The dragon-like creature had breath as hot as steam and the heat tired the young prince. He gritted his teeth and kept on fighting, using his shield to keep the creature at bay while he slashed at its feet and legs.

A lucky, scything blow sliced partway through one of the creature's hamstrings. It stumbled and dropped the stone club it held, the club landing on its other foot. The pain distracted it long enough for Loric to change tack and deliver an underhand slice to the creature's jaw, following up with a kick.

The creature flew backward, landing hard on a chest and its lower jaw skimmed through the air, hitting the back of Grimhelm's head.

"Oi! Be careful Laddie, ye couldna hae known I were finished wi' ma opponent," the dwarf yelled.

"Sorry Grim." Loric grinned as he dashed forward and put the creature out of its misery. *This is just like the last melee at the Franieren Court Joust. It's just a lot more serious...* ichor flooded out of the wound, and he grimaced. *...and definitely a lot gorier.*

A blade whistled over Loric's head to sprout from the eye socket of another creature to Loric's left.

"Concentrate, Loric! That one would have had your head," Thiert called as he stabbed another through the throat.

"Thanks," the prince grunted and spun on one creature who had managed to creep up behind Silvertree. "Oh no you don't." He thrust and managed to slide the point of his blade through the armhole of the breastplate the thing was wearing.

The mage threw a sprinkling of red powder over the creature in front of him. As the powder touched the creature's skin it hissed and the creature shrieked in pain, throwing its weapon down and trying to escape from the room.

Grimhelm ended that ambition by smashing the thing's skull in with Bessie. By the time the last creature laid leaking green plasma over the scattered gold, the party was exhausted and looked as battered as they felt.

"There couldn't possibly be any more creatures left," Loric panted, using a strip of his tunic to bandage a nasty gash in his leg, inflicted by one of the Dark Mistresses. It looked swollen and had a slight green tinge to the edges. *I hope Kalytia wakes up and heals this before my leg drops off.*

"The stories don't say how many inhabitants a dungeon had. Just that the Aracan Katuvana had minions enough to blacken the land with death." Silvertree leaned on his staff, draining another mana potion.

"Well, what do we do now?" Thiert snapped. "I can't get up to fight properly without bringing the whole dungeon's creatures down on us. Loric and Grimhelm are seriously hurt, Kalytia is still fast asleep and Silvertree is almost out of mana."

"You have a point, thief," Grimhelm replied, dropping to sit on a chest filled with gold. "I cannae do much more wi'oot a rest o'some sort."

"What do you suggest, Thiert?" Loric asked.

"I think we should arrange ourselves around Kalytia." He gestured towards the corner. "Create a barricade out of chests, and then I'll get up and jump over. Hopefully, I'll make it before anything else lands on us that could possibly be in this place. Including the Devil Demon

Silvertree said he saw," Thiert sighed. "Then we hope to the Light that we can survive long enough to get away again."

"It's as good a plan as any we've tried so far, Loric," Grimhelm said, standing up and hefting the chest he had been sitting on. He stumped over to Kalytia and wedged it between two other chests and went back for another.

Silvertree moved behind the growing wall and drank another mana potion, clearly preparing himself for whatever would be next.

Loric dragged three large gilded shields over to lie in front of the chests and located a few pieces of armour for himself. He did offer some to Thiert, but the thief refused them.

"I fight better unencumbered."

Loric shrugged and slipped a steel breastplate over his scale coat and Grimhelm found a helm filled with diamonds, which he emptied out and tossed over to the prince.

Loric retrieved the knife Thiert had used to save his life and handed it to the thief.

"Thanks. Um, Loric," Thiert looked unhappy.

"Yes?"

"That favour you promised me. I'd like to redeem it now."

"All right. What did you want me to do?"

"If I start doing anything strange or the tattoo starts changing colour..."

"Yes?"

"Kill me."

Loric blinked. "Are you sure?"

"I would rather die, than become one of the Aracan Katuvana's followers. Please Loric?"

"All right. I'll make it quick." The Prince sighed. *I know he's a criminal, but I feel sorry for him. I hope I don't have to do it.*

"Thank you." The thief seemed a lot happier as he cleaned the plasma off the blade of the knife with a nearby tapestry.

After a few more minutes, the four of them finally felt prepared. Silvertree readied a shield spell and Grimhelm joined Loric behind the chests. Thiert took a deep breath and sat up carefully, sliding his knives out. Everyone else seemed to stop breathing as the thief shifted his weight onto his feet and stood up.

There was a long silence and just for that moment, Loric thought their luck had changed. Thiert took three steps towards them; a massive Ruby tumbled down the pile, bounced on the top of the trap and rolled away towards the south west corner.

Thiert took another two steps before the alarm erupted into a cacophony of sound and light, a screeching, wailing noise that ranged along every pitch known to man, accompanied by flashing blue and red lights.

All three doors slammed open, but no creatures came through. The trap continued to scream. Thiert dove behind the barricade and Silvertree activated a shield spell, attaching it to the fortification.

After ten minutes the trap stopped wailing, although the flashing continued.

Loric could see through the south door from his position and there, floating in the centre of a carved dais, throbbing and glowing like a small red sun, was the crystal he had come to get.

"Grim!" he hissed.

"What is it, Lad?"

"There's the Heart Crystal. How about we grab it and get out of here?"

Grimhelm peered around his charge. "It doesnae appear to be guarded; we might be able ta pull it off." He sounded uncertain.

Thiert whispered. "I'll get it."

"It's my Crystal!" Loric protested.

"Who's the thief around here? Besides, I'm expendable."

"Be careful." Loric said. I don't like this. It's too easy to get to; like we're being dared to try.

Thiert rolled his eyes and slid round behind Loric and out of the barricade. He pulled a soft cotton bag from a belt pouch and crept towards the Crystal.

Loric couldn't breathe.

Thiert crept up the stairs and with a swift swipe of his bag, covered the Crystal and tried to pull it down. "It won't move!" he hissed.

"Try again," Loric replied, edging towards the side of the barricade. Grimhelm grabbed his belt and tugged him back.

Thiert tried again, bracing himself against one of the four gilded, scale carved arms that surrounded the Heart Crystal. He stopped breathing heavily. "It's no use, I can't move it."

"I've had enough!" Loric snapped. "There are no more creatures coming and if I can get that Crystal and get it home to Galindren, my father will have no choice but to name me the Official Heir to the throne. Then I might be able to stop him from carrying out whatever mad plan he's cooked up in the time we've been away."

He pulled away from Grimhelm and scrambled out from behind the barricade. Joining Thiert on the dais, he examined the arms.

"I wonder what's holding the Crystal up. There aren't any tethers or wires."

A small grey figure whizzed around the dais. Loric and Thiert jumped.

"T'is only a Golem, Lad." Grimhelm called. "Ye're tutor felt there may be some magic involved."

Loric breathed again and looked at Silvertree.

"There's a force field, Highness. Break the arms and the Heart Crystal will fall," the elven mage said.

Thiert nodded and agreed. "That would explain it."

He went back into the treasure room and returned with a pair of war hammers with jewelled collars. "Here, use this." He handed one to Loric.

"Thanks."

The two of them started smashing at the arms from opposite sides. It made a terrible noise that echoed around the room. Grimhelm came out from behind the barricade.

"I think ye must be right about there being no more creatures, Lad, ye're making enough noise to disturb Lady Hel in t'Underworld," he said, hefting Bessie. "Let me gi'e ye a hand, so we can be out o' here quickly."

Between the three of them, the first arm started to crack. Then it crumbled into a pile of rubble. Thiert and Loric tried to move the Crystal to no avail.

"Let's break another arm," Loric suggested.

"What if it summons that devil demon?" Silvertree called as he came out from behind the barricade.

"We only have your word that it exists, Silvertree." Loric grunted as his hammer rebounded.

"Are you saying that you don't trust me anymore?"

"I didn't say that. You could have seen an illusion created by another trap."

"Illusions don't see through and break spells."

"Whatever. Give us a hand, would you! The faster we get this Crystal…"

"Very well." Silvertree grumbled. He raised his staff and spoke a word. A fireball slammed into the arm and exploded with a massive concussion of sound.

"Right, we'll do this methodically," Grimhelm instructed, "Silvertree shoots a fireball, and then each of us hits the arm after it. That should bring it down faster."

The three of them hammered, and then paused for the next fireball. It disintegrated almost as soon as the fireball touched it. But the crystal still didn't budge when Loric tried to move it.

A BEGINNING

"Let's just take out the other two arms." Loric started pounding at the third arm, Thiert and Grimhelm joining him, but when they paused for the fireball it didn't materialise.

"Silvertree what happened to the..." Loric turned to look at the elven mage, "By Tyr's Beard!"

The mage had a shimmering force field around him, and warlocks filled the whole treasure room.

Loric and Thiert dropped the hammers and drew their swords.

Grimhelm charged in, yelling in Dwarfish and soon the air teemed with spraying blood and screaming Warlocks.

Silvertree watched helplessly until Loric killed the warlock shielding him, then he shouted at the top of his voice "*Ndengina!*"

The surviving Warlocks dropped to the floor, clutching their heads in their hands, blood pouring from eye sockets, ears and nose.

Silvertree collapsed and Loric caught him.

The mage coughed slightly and looked surprised when his hand came away from his mouth bloody. "Ah."

"You used the rest of your mana?" Loric asked laying the elf down carefully beside the barricade around Kalytia.

Silvertree nodded.

"Even the reserve amount to keep your heart beating?"

Silvertree sighed and coughed, his blood bubbling and trickling from his mouth and nose. "Sorry."

"Nothing to apologise for. I'll tell your Family of your bravery myself." Loric bit his lower lip, holding back the tears that threatened to overwhelm him. *This isn't right. No one was supposed to die, we were just supposed to get the crystal and go home to Galindren as heroes.*

Silvertree smiled weakly. "Loric?"

"Yes?"

"This wasn't your fault. I have suspected for a while that there was something controlling your father, before you even mentioned the golden ring in his eyes. This—adventure—just confirms that you were sent here deliberately." The mage coughed and blood flooded from his mouth.

The prince turned the mage's head, sensing that Silvertree wanted to say something else important.

As the flow became a trickle, Silvertree looked up into Loric's eyes, his leaf green eyes holding the prince's blue ones. "Tell my wife I love her."

Loric nodded. The light went from the elf's eyes and Loric gently closed his lids, feeling both angry and sad. Picking up the mage's staff and Bag of Holding, he said, "I'm beginning to think that we're not going to get out of here alive, Grim."

"Ye may be right lad," Grimhelm sniffed, blotting his eyes with the end of his beard.

Eight

Loric just had time to lay the staff and bag beside Kalytia, shift the chests around to hide her and return to the Heart Crystal's dais before another wave of creatures hit. He found himself faced with a sea of enemies. A mixture of Dark Mistresses, Dragon Spawn, Skeletons and Gremlins surged in from the doors of the dais room.

"Don't they ever just give up?" he shouted, slicing three gremlins in half with one blow.

"What d'ye think, Laddie, that they were gonna just let ye take the crystal?" Grimhelm laughed. "Besides, do ye no feel alive, the rage o'battle fillin' ye're veins?"

Loric rolled his eyes and beheaded a skeleton. The thing's body wandered away toward the dwarf who smashed the bones apart gleefully.

Thiert dashed and darted through the morass of creatures, his poniard slipping through chinks in armour and piercing vulnerable throats. He moved so fast that the prince lost sight of him from one moment to the next.

They fought automatically, killing each creature as fast as possible before moving on to the next. By the time the tide began to ebb from the doors, they had gathered in front of where Kalytia lay, in a slow retreat.

A dragon creature slipped in under Grimhelm's guard and savaged the dwarf's leg, ripping the sturdy muscle to shreds and cracking the bone with a sickening sound which carried over the surrounding noise.

Grimhelm grunted and caved the thing's skull in. "Ye cannae stop me, lads!" he crowed. "I'll take twice the number down before I fall, and I'll kill three times more from the ground."

Thiert seemed to have a knack with the Dark Mistresses; he feinted with one hand and while they followed the feint, sliced through their throats with practised ease with the other. "I thought these women were supposed to be intelligent?" he called to Loric.

"Don't ask me, Silvertree was the one who knew about them," the prince called back as he hacked and slashed his way through the skeletons and gremlins. "Try and move back to the dais room."

The other two nodded in acknowledgement and the three warriors began to press their foes forward again, accelerating their individual skirmishes so they could advance.

By the time they reached the dais, a carpet of bodies lay around them, some still spurting bodily fluids, others breathing their last. Loric looked around. *This is absolute carnage, who on earth would throw away their followers like this?*

A lone Gremlin stood in the doorway, its pupil-less eyes blinking as it breathed hard from exertion.

Loric raised his blood drenched sabre and took a step towards the tiny creature. The Gremlin screamed, dropped its dagger and ran away shouting at the top of its voice. "Retreat, retreat! Evacuate the dungeon!"

Loric leaned back against the second dais arm breathing heavily. Grimhelm sat groaning on the bottom step, his right leg broken and useless. Thiert was the only person still with any energy.

He attacked the third arm and surprisingly all the arms dissolved, tipping Loric onto the dais as the magic field around the Heart Crystal stopped working and dropped, still inside the bag Thiert had put on it.

Loric caught the bag and grinned at Thiert.

"Thank you, my friend."

"I'm a thief. I'm no one's friend." Thiert's answering grin was broad and made Loric laugh.

"Come on, Grim. Let's grab Kalytia and get out of here," Loric said using his hilt to push himself up.

A BEGINNING

The Dwarf said nothing.

"Grim? Grimhelm?" Loric spun round to see Thiert pull one of his knives out from under the dwarf's chin. "What are you are doing?!"

"I told you. I'm no one's friend." The thief replied softly, wiping his knife on his trousers.

Loric stared at him, panic rising in his chest. In front of his eyes, the thief's tattoo transformed from black to full colour, with blood red roses blooming between the thorns. "Thiert, snap out of it man!"

The little thief looked at him, his eyes bright gold from edge to pupil.

"You come into my dungeon; you kill my creatures and plunder my treasure. Then you steal my Heart Crystal, and you think that you can get away with it?" the man laughed, but it was the laugh of a Demon, deep and hollow, echoing around the room.

"But, the Black Tower War! All the stories say the Dungeons were cleansed," Loric said.

"Hah! I am Aracan Katuvana, and it is time that you puny humans with your soft, delicate bodies and delicious spirits realised that I will never be destroyed." Thiert's face began to change as his skin darkened.

Loric dropped the bag holding the Heart Crystal onto the dais and moved around it towards Thiert, holding his blade out in front of him.

"Release Thiert and I will leave your Crystal and your dungeon alone."

The little man didn't move, he just waited, a sardonic smile on his face. When the point of the Sabre touched his chest just over the heart, he laughed.

"You cannot kill me, boy."

From this close, Loric could see the centre of the gold eyes were still deep blue.

"There is still something human in there," Loric said softly.

"This man is mine. He has been mine since he was born, everything he has told you has been a lie and at my command," the Demon possessing Thiert told Loric.

"I would rather die than become one of the Aracan Katuvana's followers. Please Loric." Thiert's voice whispered in Loric's mind and as he looked at the rogue, he saw in the little blue centre, the calm of a man prepared to die.

He swallowed with difficulty.

"Do you really think you can prevail against my Power?" the possessing demon hissed.

"Yes, actually, I do," Loric replied and taking a swift step forward, he thrust his sabre into the man's heart, just the first four inches of the blade, but he could have sworn he felt the bone at the back grate against the point as it slid through the heart.

A red mist rose from the body and vanished with a crash of imploding air as the possession spell was broken.

I hope that really hurts the bastard. Loric thought, remembering the agony Silvertree had been in when his Golem Snake was destroyed.

The thief's chest heaved as he tried to hold onto life. "Thank you my friend. I hope you manage to get the end you desire from all of this death." The thief whispered.

"I'm actually beginning to wonder if it's just my father that's insane," Loric replied.

The thief smiled, as he took a shallow breath. "Nothing in this life is sane." He wheezed.

Loric forced a laugh. "That's one way of looking at it." The light left Thiert's eyes.

Stepping back, he pulled the blade out.

Turning, Loric fell to his knees beside the body and saw that Thiert's eyes had returned to the deep blue he remembered. He closed the thief's eyelids and wiped a thread of blood from his cheek.

"Now what?" Loric asked himself. "I suppose I should get Kalytia out of here. She, at least, does not deserve to die in this place." His voice echoed through the rooms, and he shivered.

Gathering Grimhelm's war hammer and the clan amulet from around his neck, Loric slipped them into the little money bag Grimhelm had been using and tied the bag to his belt.

He looked at the thief's body and frowned.

"Should I take your bag too?" he asked it. "Well, the Trap Hunter might come in handy, and I don't think you'd mind," he answered himself as he untied it from Thiert's belt and added it to his. *Now I know I'm going mad, talking to dead people.*

Picking up the crystal from the dais, he went back to where Kalytia lay. He fed Silvertree's staff into the elf's Bag of Holding, then slung it over his shoulder, before turning to the sleeping woman. Gently, Loric shook her awake.

Kalytia roused slowly. "What's going on, Loric?" she mumbled.

She's still sleepy. It does sound good to hear my name on her lips, though. He bit back a smile at the thought.

"We have to get out of here, Lady Cleric. Silvertree, Grimhelm and Thiert are dead, and I must warn my Father of the danger posed by the Black Tower and its Aracan Katuvana."

The news brought her all the way awake and she scrambled to her feet. "Have you done what you came to do, your Highness?"

"Yes, Lady."

"Then I shall mourn our friends later, when we have time." She looked at his wounds carefully and using her statuette, she healed them as if they were never there. "The blessing of My Lady be upon you, your Highness."

He bowed his head. "Thank you, Lady Cleric."

The two left the Treasure room into the now paved and fortified corridor with skeletal hands holding torches every few feet.

"Hmm. Maybe we ought to be a bit more careful now," Loric said. "Looks like they've had the place done up."

Kalytia nodded. "Have you got the Trap Hunter?"

Loric fished around in Thiert's pack and brought out the device. In his hand it just looked like a dull grey sphere. He handed it to Kalytia, who looked at it carefully, then whispered something in Elvish to it. The Trap Hunter glowed orange and Kalytia smiled.

"Eliethor always uses common Elvish for general items." She giggled. "I wonder…" she whispered another Elvish word and the Trap Hunter glowed yellow and lifted from her palm, hovering in front of her.

"I thought so. It has a second setting," Kalytia sighed. "Poor Thiert, if he'd known about the automatic setting, he wouldn't have needed to do so much work."

Loric gave her a sad smile. "Come on, Lady Cleric."

"Your Highness, we have known each other since before I entered the temple and we have participated in many adventures together." Kalytia looked at him through her eyelashes, "Maybe it's time that we became a little less formal with each other?"

"What are you suggesting?" Loric's heart leaped in his chest, making him feel breathless.

"Well, you could drop the Lady Cleric in private for a start." She grinned at him.

"Only if you drop the Your Highness as well. I do have a name, as you well know." He took a step toward her.

"It would be good to be friends again, Loric." She said.

"We never stopped being friends, Kalytia." He took another step, "I'd like to be more than that to you."

She shook her head. "You know that I am wedded to the Goddess, Loric."

He sighed. "I had hoped…"

A BEGINNING

Taking a step, she took his face in both hands. "Hope is a good thing, but in this case friendship is all I can offer you as I am." She kissed him lightly on the lips to take the sting of her words away and was surprised by the feeling it gave her. She leaned into the kiss more and her breath seemed to halt.

Loric resisted the temptation to pull her to him and make the kiss into more. He pulled away gently and smiled. "There will be time to explore the options later, my Lady. For now, we must escape the dungeon and return home."

Kalytia nodded, catching her breath.

Loric took her hand and they moved swiftly down the corridor together, the Trap Hunter hovering over the floor a few feet in front of them as they moved. The pair was forced to pause at the torture chamber as the Trap Hunter revealed three spike traps arranged in a row in front of them. Kalytia disarmed them with a quick prayer.

"I didn't know you could do that." Loric said.

"Neither did I, I just asked for help; obviously My Goddess is watching." She made the symbol of Espilieth in the air in front of her.

Does that mean that the Goddess was watching her kiss me? Does she approve? Could I... he stopped that train of thought and suggested that they move on.

Kalytia agreed.

They encountered no resistance for the rest of the way, just the occasional Gremlin that would run screaming back the way they appeared from.

At the end of the new corridor a horde of skeletons blocked their way. Loric rolled his shoulders and drew his sword. "Stay behind me, Kalytia."

She shook her head. "No, you will need someone to watch your back." She drew her holy blade, it's white glow reflecting from the grey stones and dulling the light from the torches on the walls.

"Very well but be careful, I couldn't bear losing another friend." He touched her arm, "Especially you."

The skeletons attacked. Loric concentrated on smashing them into pieces so that he gained breathing space as the bones reformed. However, the animated bones crumbled into dust at the touch of Kalytia's blade, and recognising this, they fell into a rhythm. Loric would knock the skeleton to pieces and Kalytia would turn it to dust as it reformed.

Soon there was nothing left of their attackers but drifts of dust. They put their weapons away and began moving again.

Kalytia looked around as they entered the next corridor. "I can feel... something."

"What?" Loric asked, taking her hand again. *I like the feel of her hand in mine. It feels... right.*

"Evil."

"You said that the whole place was evil." He replied as they walked down toward the door.

"It is. This is different, a more solid kind of evil." She shrugged, "It makes me want to run."

"Then run we shall." Loric said.

There were no more creatures, no skeletons or even gremlins. The traps they found were easily disarmed.

It made Loric feel uneasy. *We're being played with, I know it.*

"It's too straightforward," He panted as they ran around the corner towards the main entrance.

Kalytia nodded.

At the main entrance, the Trap Hunter indicated that these traps had been reset. Kalytia had to use more mana to disarm them, and the alarm trap took the longest to disarm.

"I see why Lord Silvertree wanted Thiert along," she said as they slipped out the door. "If I didn't have a constant mana source from my Goddess, I'd be almost dead by now."

Loric had a sudden flash back to the moment his friend and tutor had died, blinking away tears. *No time to mourn now, we have to get out of here!*

Nine

At the crossroads the traps were also active, and they had to waste valuable minutes disarming them. Loric waited impatiently, sabre at the ready while Kalytia removed the threat from each one.

"I can't defuse the gas trap, Loric," she hissed back to him. "The mechanism is too complex."

"Put your mask on, hold your breath for as long as possible and we'll run through," Loric suggested.

She nodded and pulled the red mask from her bag, swiftly tying the straps in place. She held the bag with the crystal while Loric fastened his.

"Right then," he said, "one, two, and three..."

They dashed through the centre of the crossroads, the Trap Hunter following them, and barely got two steps out the other side of the trap before collapsing.

Luckily, the gas was light and when they dropped close to the floor where there was a less contaminated breathing space, the masks protected them, and they could crawl away from the poison cloud.

Once free of the choking mist, Kalytia healed them, and they made their way to the beginning of the main corridor.

"Three traps to go," she sighed as the Trap Hunter located them.

"You clear them and take the crystal out of the dungeon," Loric told her. "The stories all say once the Heart Crystal is outside, the dungeon will die, and all the creatures will be destroyed."

"What about you?"

"I'll guard your back. It's been too easy to get here, so I think there is one last assault being planned." He looked back up the corridor toward the crossroads. "Can you still feel that solid evil?"

A BEGINNING

She nodded. "It's a lot closer than before and it feels... smug, as if its certain that we won't escape it."

Loric gave her the three bags of holding that he had brought from Silvertree, Grimhelm and Thiert's bodies. "Take these. If I don't get out of here alive, take Grimhelm's and Silvertree's to their families. Donate Thiert's riches to a Temple of Light and take the Crystal to my Father. Tell him how I died and that Aracan Katuvana is making a bid for the Heart Kingdoms again."

Kalytia's green eyes widened, and tears began to slide down her smooth pale cheeks. "Loric..."

"Just do it, Kalytia!" Loric snapped. *I can't do this if she cries. I won't be able to fight whatever is coming if my feelings for her get the better of me.*

"Yes, Lady Cleric of Espilieth, you do that." A deep voice said from behind them and Loric spun bringing his sabre up defensively. "You take the Heart Crystal, and your precious prince dies."

From a cloud of steam that seemed to appear out of nowhere, stepped the biggest demon Loric had seen yet; three times the height of the Gas Demons they had fought earlier.

It had bright red skin and shaggy fur covered legs ending in polished black, cloven hooves. Its upper body rippled with well-toned muscles and above that, a handsome human face was topped by massive black horns that scraped the ceiling. The Devil Demon looked down on the two humans with a broad grin that Loric recognised.

"You!" he gasped.

The bright gold, pupil-less eyes curved as the Demon burst out laughing.

"Did you really think that I would let you escape mortal?" the deep voice asked, "My power is beyond anything that you puny runts could imagine."

Kalytia began praying in Elvish. A bright white light surrounded Loric, and she turned back to neutralising the traps.

"A Holy Barrier? Do you really think that will save him? Oh, how sweet." the demon asked her, but she ignored it, working swiftly on each trap and moving forward as soon as it was safe, trusting that Loric could survive long enough to escape as well.

Loric felt the blessing of Espilieth as the white light surrounded him. The exhaustion he had been feeling lifted. "Cower, Demon!" he shouted, "for I shall be your undoing!"

The Devil Demon laughed.

"So predictable. You heroes never learn," as he swung a huge scythe round in front of him. The blade gleamed evilly in the blessing's light and struck blue sparks from the paving as it cut a fine line into the stones.

"Hurry, Kalytia!" Loric yelled and raised his sabre. "Come on then, Demon."

The Demon swung its weapon as Kalytia finished the last trap and opened the door.

"Come on, Loric!" she screamed and threw herself out into the morning sunlight.

She waited for what seemed like hours and finally Loric appeared at the top of the steps, dragging himself along the floor. She dropped the bags in the light and rushed to him.

"Loric? Highness?" she said softly.

"He got me Kalytia," the prince said.

She looked back over his body and held back a scream. From mid-thigh he had nothing there. A thick trail of blood led back into the dungeon, pumping in great gouts from the wounds.

Kalytia began to pray as she had never prayed before and the blood slowed and stopped. *Lady Goddess heal him; Espilieth hear my prayer and save him. I... I... please just save him!*

That deep, sardonic laugh disrupted her train of thought and Kalytia looked back into the darkness. She saw a pair of golden pupil-less eyes with her face reflected in them. The reflection was different to the one she saw in her hand mirror every morning, the green eyes murky, tainted with unholy desire and the blonde hair brassy and dull.

"See the beauty that your goddess hides you from." the demon sneered. "See how you would be without the light she shines on you. Are you truly worthy of her notice?"

Kalytia caught her breath. *I am ugly inside.*

"Come, Lady Cleric, renounce your goddess and her fake splendour. Join me and see your true beauty shine." The taunt became soft and appealing. "I can give you what you desire."

Kalytia saw her tainted reflection brighten, the hair curling effortlessly and softly around her face, her eyes shining jade with light and purpose from skin as smooth as silk. On one cheek a blood red rose bloomed between black thorns and deep red lips parted provocatively.

Her hand rose toward her face, eyes widening with wonder. *I could look so much more...attractive.*

"You could have anything that you desire... even your princeling." The voice continued and an image entered her mind, of her and Loric sat upon the thrones of Galivor with matching crowns; of the two of them in bed together, passionate kisses and movements hidden under a red silk coverlet.

She gasped as her body responded to the image and her heart began to pound. *But I gave that up when I entered the temple, I should not feel this... it is unseemly for one such as I to...*

The demon crooned, sensing her weakness. "Come to me, Lovely Lady. I shall give you such pleasure that you will never want to leave my side." He leaned the scythe against the wall and held his hands out to her.

"Kalytia." Loric tugged on her cloak, and she looked down into his blue eyes. "Don't give in. You are worth more than all the pleasure in the world."

The face she saw reflected in his eyes was more exquisite than the one she saw in her mirror. *What is it he sees that I don't?*

"It is his love for you." the Goddess whispered in her mind and for a moment, Kalytia felt Espilieth's hand touch her shoulder. The cleric straightened. *"He sees you as I see you, good and holy and beautiful. You are more than worthy of your honours in my eyes."*

As the Goddess' presence left her mind, Kalytia smiled, feeling stronger. She looked back at the demon. "No."

A laugh echoed out of the passageway. "Go then, Lady Cleric. Tell the Four Kingdoms what is approaching them. Tell them that My Master has returned," the demon said as it approached the entrance. Its eyes had black slit pupils now.

Not possessed anymore; it's just an ordinary devil demon now. She sighed, feeling a little disappointed. *I wonder what would have happened if I had taken the demon lord up on his offer?*

"The crystal, Kalytia, expose the crystal to sunlight!" Loric said weakly "It will collapse the dungeon."

She shook her thoughts aside and scrambled up, grabbing the bag with the crystal. "I will do it, Demon!"

"I care not what you do, mortal. I may not be able to stand in the sunlight at the moment, but once Aracan Katuvana triumphs over Galivor, the rest of the kingdoms shall fall, and I shall exit the underground to ride with him to victory!"

"I shall never allow that to come to pass!" Kalytia shouted and opened the neck of the bag.

The sunlight flooded into the bag and the crystal pulsed red one last time. Then the colour faded, and the crystal turned a cloudy white. The ground beneath them shook and Kalytia ran back, dragging Loric out of the way as the entrance crashed down. She caught one more glimpse of the Devil Demon before it teleported away, and the tunnel filled with rubble.

A BEGINNING

KALYTIA COMPLETED HER report of the adventure to King Koric in a flat tone. *It still hurts, will it ever stop hurting?* She hoped this was one of his saner moments.

She was wrong.

"You are lying," he said calmly.

"I swear on the name of the Goddess Espilieth that I tell the truth, your Majesty," she replied, noticing that Loric's brother, Korin looked uncomfortable.

The King looked down at the Heart Crystal on the table in front of her and pointed to it.

"Korin. Bring that to me."

Korin nodded and the young man stepped down from the dais to pick up the Crystal. His eyes widened as he saw Loric's signet ring on her finger.

"Is that Loric's...?"

"Yes, your Highness. He gave it to me with his dying breath and asked that I tell you something." She lowered her voice.

"What?"

"These were his exact words: 'Tell Korin that I swear by the statue of Fiörna our Mother gave him. Everything she says is true. Do not trust our Father with this. As I die I lay this charge on you, Brother ... stop this evil from happening. Do what you must to destroy the Heart Crystals in every dungeon that exists." A tear ran down her cheek at the memory.

Korin turned back to look at his Father and realised something had changed about him. He whispered to Kalytia as he picked up the crystal.

"Look at my Father's eyes. Is there anything different?"

She did as asked, and her own eyes widened with horror.

"He is possessed, your Highness. He has the gold and black eyes of the Devil Demon."

"That's what I thought. Run, Lady Cleric, and if I survive the next few minutes, I will meet you in the Temple of Light. I swear this by my brother's ring." Korin turned his back on her, and she bolted.

The King frowned. "Why did she run? I am not going to hurt her."

"I told her to, Father," Korin replied.

"Ah well. No matter, bring the crystal here, Son. You are my Heir now."

Korin stopped a step below the throne and looked at his father's Lord Steward beside the throne, hoping that the man wouldn't try to stop him. A slight narrowing of the Steward's eyes and an even slighter nod made him feel better.

"Do you acknowledge me as your official heir, Father?"

"You are my only living heir. Of course, that makes you my official heir."

Korin didn't move and the greedy expression on his father's face darkened.

"All right! I name you, Prince Korin, last living son of my late wife Princess Selestiale of Jira, my Official and only Heir to the Kingdom of Galivor." The King glared, "Happy now?"

"Well, Lord Garonne?" Korin looked at the Lord Steward again.

The man nodded and smiled at him.

"Thank you, Father. The Lady Cleric communicated a message to me from my brother. I believe everything she has told us, and I will do all that is in my power to carry out the instructions Loric gave me with his last breath."

"Very well, son. I will allow you to carry out your brother's wishes. Just give me the crystal!"

Korin looked at his Father and swallowed against the tears that threatened his composure.

A BEGINNING

"Lord Garonne. By the Power vested in me as Heir to the Kingdom of Galivor, I declare my Father, King Koric of Galivor, insane. I therefore declare my intentions to do as my ancestor Kervic did three hundred years ago."

The Lord Steward nodded.

Korin turned, throwing the crystal onto the flagstones. It shattered and the escaping magic turned the shards to dust. The magic drew the dust upward into the shape of the Tower and Eye symbol, before dispersing. The magic's theatrics had drawn the gaze of everyone in the hall and before the guards had time to react, Korin drew his sword and beheaded his father.

The body toppled from the throne. The head bounced down the steps to land with the face upward. The eyes blinked and Korin saw they were entirely gold now.

The lips moved.

"Do you truly think that you can stand against Aracan Katuvana of The Black Tower, Princeling?" the head said in a deep booming voice that echoed around the room.

"As King of Galivor, I stand ready to repel you, Evil One," Korin answered.

"Then look not to your borders, but to your lands, Princeling. For I shall carpet Galivor with the bodies of the fallen." The eyes returned to brown and Korin choked back tears. *Farewell Father. Farewell Loric. I will save our Kingdom; that I promise you.*

"WELL, THAT WENT BETTER than could be expected, milord!" the Jar chuckled from its stand as Aracan Katuvana returned to his throne. "One dungeon down, but easily replaceable, as long as I...you act quickly. Korin will need time to consolidate his hold upon his kingdom before he carries out Loric's wishes."

The Aracan sat down and nodded.

"It's a pity that you couldn't persuade the Cleric to join us, she was clearly very powerful and would have made an excellent High Priestess of the Dark Temple." The Jar said licking its lips, "I would have enjoyed indoctrinating her into the practices required."

Grunting, the Aracan thumped the arm of the chair, but the Jar had been carried away by its own fancy and its voice rippled with blood lust. "The four Kingdoms shall be yours once more, death and destruction shall blanket the lands, blood shall run in the waters and evil will breathe air untainted by goodness once more."

The Aracan Katuvana nodded again and leaned against the throne's tall back. He stopped moving completely, just the gentle rise and fall of his chest showing that he was still, if he had ever been, alive.

"Sleep well, Lord." The Jar murmured. "And when you wake I...we shall begin my...our return."

Author Note

Dear Readers,

Thank you for sticking with me long enough to get this far!

I started writing seriously in 2011. At the time I thought it was easy enough to do (well, compared to Teaching) and I had a lot of fun messing around with short stories and poetry and learning to discard the rules I'd learned at school.

The Tower and The Eye emerged from my love of Fantasy, Sword & Sorcery, Table top Role Playing Gaming and various console and computer games. The story that you have just read is, at its core, a homage to the genre. You may have recognised some of the influences as you read through.

This one story spawned a second, based on a TTRPG game that I had tried to run over the internet with some friends. While the game didn't get past the initial encounter and set up, it helped me to bring another story to life in the same world.

After I completed the second book, I had to stop to get some world building done and that in itself helped me to continue and complete the series, which was picked up by several small press publishers, one after the other. All of the editors helped me to improve the stories, and most recently, some extensive feedback brought me to create this, the latest edition.

It couldn't have come to pass without the support and encouragement of many different people. So, without further ado, please allow me to thank:

My very first Patrons, Sammy Smith and Maggie Stewart Grant; the lovely people of the World of the Teigr Princess (my beta reading group); Elizabeth Bank for her Cover Design skills; the editing skills of Diane Nelson and Kristen Stone, the unwavering support of my friends from the Third Person Group and last, but not in the bit least, the love and encouragement of my family...

And now to reward your patience, over the page you will find a sneak peek into the second book of The Tower and The Eye: A Party at Castle Grof.

TTFN,

K

Excerpt
A Party at Castle Grof

Book Two of The Tower and the Eye

Castle Grof has claimed the lives of many already, but Lord Harnez of Valdez is determined to clear the menace of the dungeon underneath the ruins completely.

Drawn into the quest with a barbarian warrior, a monk of Tyr and an old friend, Aranok and his half-sister, Ariana, begin to wonder if they will actually return to their home in the elven realm of Alethdariel alive...

"WHAT DO YOU THINK YOU'RE doing, Erendell?" Ariana yelled.

"Aranok said it was taking too long, so I decided to speed things up a little," the half Drow said in an unconcerned manner.

"You idiot, Erendell, there's a guard post behind the wall! They're..." The Mech broke through the last of the wall. Behind it stood four massive, two headed dogs, drool dripping from between their six inch fangs as they growled at the party from atop a wooden platform.

"...waiting for us." Ariana shook her head ruefully. She deactivated the Mech with a flick of a finger and a small magic pressure before it could start to dig into the platform.

Erendell backed up quickly and bumped into Grald. The barbarian dropped Arnhammen to the floor and spun to catch the elf as she fell. Aranok jumped back to avoid being knocked over. Grald set Erendell back on her feet and moved back slightly, loosening his sword in his scabbard.

"What the...?" Aranok asked, glancing between the Hell Hound and Ariana.

"No time now, Brother, we need to get out of here!" she replied, turning to run back down the tunnel.

"Going somewhere?" a voice drawled languidly from the shadows.

Arnhammen scrambled up and hurled himself between the surprised mage and the rest of the tunnel.

Ariana produced a mage globe and lit it with a gesture. It flared bright white and lit the whole tunnel revealing a figure wearing luxurious, deep red velvet, in the form of a hooded robe, its face in hidden by the shadow.

"That's a little too bright, young human," the voice said. "Here, let me dim it for you." The figure made a motion with a gloved hand and the mage globe changed to a pale yellow light. "That's much better."

Aranok found that he couldn't move. Neither could Ariana, Erendell or Grald.

Arnhammen pulled his mace from its sling and growled, "Get ye gone from this place, Unholy One. Get ye gone in Tyr's name, lest ye taste His Wrath through mine Holy Mace!"

As the dwarf invoked Tyr's name, he struck the weapon against the floor, and it burst into deep blue flames. The figure shrank back from the mace as Arnhammen advanced on it and the hood on the robe fell back, revealing the figure's face.

Aranok gasped "Liana!"

"No, Half Human. I am the Lych Mistress, Custodian of this Dungeon that you shall soon languish in," the elven woman replied harshly. "Seize them!"

Around them ten women appeared, all dressed in skimpy, tight leather battle harness with steel tipped, high-heeled boots. They seemed to have no weapons, but their long fingernails were filed into points and their long hair was plaited and tipped with blades.

"Ye shall never take us, Unholy One, for no matter who ye be, the power of Tyr be far greater!" Arnhammen roared and charged at the Lych Mistress.

Four of the women dove on the dwarf and he bashed them away like so many flies at the end of a horse's tail. They slammed up against the walls of the tunnel, disturbing the solidifying spell so that earth crumbled around them. The women screeched, showing sharpened teeth.

Arnhammen ignored them and attacked the Lych Mistress again. This time his mace made contact and the elven woman screeched and disappeared in a flash of blue light...

Don't miss out!

Visit the website below and you can sign up to receive emails whenever Kira Morgana publishes a new book. There's no charge and no obligation.

https://books2read.com/r/B-A-SVI-FDJVB

BOOKS 2 READ

Connecting independent readers to independent writers.

Also by Kira Morgana

Terrene Empire Tales
Blossom & Kitsune: A Brief Tale of Earthquakes and Nine Tailed Foxes
Snow & Kitsune: A Long Tale of Wild Weather and Tanuki

The Dragon Flower Saga
Hat or Tiara?

The Secret of Arking Down
The Angel's Crown
The Dragon's Pendant
The Second Door

The Tower and The Eye
A Beginning

Standalone

The Necklace of Harmony: A short story collection

Watch for more at tpsworld.wordpress.com.

About the Author

Kira thought she was a Teacher, until Life pointed out to her that she is actually a writer. As her Cats, Kids and Partner (in that order) approved, she decided to agree with Life.

Currently she is working on a seven book Science Fantasy series, with several accompanying spinoffs and as "A.E. Churchyard" on several Science Fiction projects.

As if that weren't enough to do, she also sings in a Chorus Line, takes Tap lessons, and is delving into the world of Illustration and Graphic Novels

She does all this from a body in South Wales, UK. Where her mind is, she hasn't yet worked out, because apart from seeing a lot of fantasy creatures, she hasn't actually managed to find someone with a connection to a map app...

Read more at tpsworld.wordpress.com.

About the Publisher

Teigr Books is the official Publisher of all Kira Morgana, A. E. Churchyard and Mandy E. Ward books.

Milton Keynes UK
Ingram Content Group UK Ltd.
UKHW051946250624
444714UK00013B/626